Silver Spoon Romeo

(book five of the Royal Romeos series)
by Jenny Gardiner

Copyright © 2017 by Jenny Gardiner
Cover art by Kim Killion, The Killion Group, Inc.

ISBN: 978-1944763077

Chapter One

SOPHIE Pellegrino had grown weary of famous people who did idiotic things. Professionally, it didn't bode well for her, considering she'd been producing a soul-exposing (and not in a good way), mea culpa-type reality show that featured celebrities who'd landed themselves in a pickle for all sorts of embarrassing reasons. Usually it was regrettable behavior induced by too much Cuervo, recreational drugs, arrogance, or a combination thereof, and sometimes it was out of sheer stupidity. Simply because you were a famous celebrity didn't mean you had a brain that served you well.

She'd produced stories about an actress found running naked down Rodeo Drive while shouting like a fishmonger that her actor boyfriend was having sex with the Dalai Lama (she claimed a bad case of exhaustion). And the famous reality TV shrink who turned out to have three families in three different countries (he chalked it up to too many anxiety meds).

Then there was the married actor and father of three who was caught on camera in a compromising position with a child star on the set of his latest film (he was a big fan of Ecstasy, both the drug and the state of). Sophie shook her head on that one, wondering what the hell was wrong with the man. Couldn't he see nothing good would come of that once he was busted? They always got caught. And that boded well for her show: there was never a dearth of sordid stories with which to regale her audience and the publicists desperate to force their clients onto her show for damage control purposes. She sometimes wondered if celebrities did some of this stuff to remain relevant, which would be sort of pathetic yet not too surprising. Sometimes those who feasted at the banquet of fame starved to death without it and were willing to settle for notoriety instead.

She was beginning to feel like she needed a long, hot soak after work each night. Not so much to relax, but rather to cleanse the figurative muck off after dealing with the many unseemly people who thought fame was a license to behave abhorrently.

That's why the timing could not have been better when her boss announced some big changes were looming.

"Soph, I've got some great news for you." Danny Slinger spoke like a human machine gun in a rapid-fire New York-accented banter as he slurped what was probably his eighth cup of high-octane coffee before noon. His mussed-up, salt-and-pepper hair hung over his eyes as if he couldn't be bothered to get it trimmed, and he was missing a button on his shirt. When around her best friends, Sophie tended to refer to Danny as a bit of a schlub since he never seemed to put a scintilla of effort into personal maintenance. Nevertheless, she respected him professionally in spades. "You're getting your own show. Starting immediately, you're going to produce and host a lifestyle program featuring fantasy destinations."

Sophie pretended to clean her ears out as if she hadn't heard him right. "Is this a joke? Cause seriously, I don't think I can handle it if you tell me in five minutes you were

What people are saying about Jenny Gardiner's books:

"A fun, sassy read! A cross between Erma Bombeck and Candace Bushnell, reading Jenny Gardiner is like sinking your teeth into a chocolate cupcake…you just want more."
--Meg Cabot, NY Times bestselling author of Princess Diaries, Queen of Babble and more, on Sleeping with Ward Cleaver

"With a strong yet delightfully vulnerable voice, food critic Abbie Jennings embarks on a soulful journey where her love for banana cream pie and disdain for ill-fitting Spanx clash in hilarious and heartbreaking ways. As her body balloons and her personal life crumbles, Abbie must face the pain and secret fears she's held inside for far too long. I cheered for her the entire way."
--Beth Hoffman, NY Times bestselling author of *Saving CeeCee Honeycutt* on *Slim to None*

"Jenny Gardiner has done it again--this fun, fast-paced book is a great summer read."
--Sarah Pekkanen, NY Times bestselling author of *The Opposite of Me*, on *Slim to None*

"As Sweet as a song and sharp as a beak, *Bite Me* really soars as a memoir about family--children and husbands, feathers and fur--and our capacity to keep loving though life may occasionally bite."
--Wade Rouse, bestselling author of At Least in the City Someone Would Hear Me Scream

just pulling my leg." She ran her fingers through her long, mahogany hair that fell in soft waves over her shoulders.

Danny took another swig of coffee, his hyper-caffeinated brain causing the mug to tremble in his hands. "Would I lie to you?"

His mouth spread into one of those annoying grins you see when your poker opponent tells you he has four Jacks to beat your full house. The kind of smug look you'd usually want to wipe off a guy's face. Only for Danny, it all worked in his favor.

"Uh, yeah," she said, her earthen brown eyes twinkling, highlighting her high cheekbones. "Remember that time you told me you'd landed that marriage-in-the-shitter Brad Pitt interview and I was going to be in charge of it?"

He rolled his eyes and slapped the heel of his hand to his forehead. "Are you that dense?" He fixed his gaze on her. "It was April Fool's Day. You should've known that was a lie. Besides, don't you think I'd have taken on someone of his magnitude if we'd actually gotten him?"

"My first clue should have been that Brangelina—minus the 'ngelina'—would never do an interview for one of your tawdry shows."

He clutched his hands to his heart. "You're killing me, Pellegrino." He half pushed her away and fake staggered a few steps. "Here I do you a solid and what do I get? Disrespect."

Sophie lifted her eyebrows in hope. "Wait, so you're telling me you're actually serious?"

"As a heart attack. Which you're going to give me if you turn this down."

"Are you kidding? I was beginning to think we needed

to install a disinfectant room to cleanse ourselves after the show, the program's turned so icky. I would love nothing more than to get away from *Gotcha* with my soul intact."

"Believe me when I say we could never have become so icky without you. Consider this your reward for a job well done. You found the bottom of the barrel and you made it look like a Park Avenue penthouse. But I do recognize it's time to let my little fledgling fly from the nest."

"You mean that shit-encrusted nest I'd have become glued to if I stayed much longer?"

"One man's bird crap is another man's Emmy award-winning programming."

Sophie tipped her head in disbelief. "Daniel Slinger, you never earned an Emmy for that program."

"I'm only saying it's possible. Just because you think my show is catering to the lowest common denominator doesn't mean that those unwashed masses who inhale every episode and obsess about it on social media for days afterward don't think the show is a class act."

Sophie rolled her eyes. "More like a class action lawsuit waiting to happen." She waved her hands as if to erase the conversation. "Enough about that. I want to hear what you've got going for me. By the way, I feel the need to get it in writing that I will never again have to interview some pathetic, attention-seeking, D-level celebrity who's just been sprung from his fourth stint in rehab after going on a joyride with a monkey at the wheel while under the influence of a controlled substance."

Danny rubbed his hands together with glee. "That was one of our best shows this year!"

"Stop!" Sophie clasped her head with her fingers,

staving off the headache that would come with him gushing about that show any more than he already had.

"Okay, okay." He held his hands up in surrender. "Here's the deal. The men in suits want to take things in a new direction. They like your style and they want to give you free rein to show us what you can do. It's going to be an aspirational type of show—your viewers are going to want to be there in your shoes. Maybe even want to kill you to replace you in those shoes."

"Like a gladiator-style show? To the death and all that?"

Danny curled his lip in annoyance. "So little faith, my dear. It's like you don't think I have your best interests at heart." He petted her head. "Trust in the process, Grasshopper."

She shook his hand away. "Sorry. It's hard to imagine instantly transitioning from the land of sludge. I can't quite fathom a world of purity and joy."

"Well, prepare yourself. Because this is your baby to do with as you please. Think about what you would love to do—put your passion behind it. And make a show out of it. Sky's the limit."

She looked skyward. "Seriously? Anything? Anywhere?"

"Within reason and within budget. Like we're not going to send you up in the space shuttle."

"Thank God."

"Give it some thought and get back to me. The executives are ready to move forward with this. I'm giving you the weekend to decide. The important thing to know is that you're in charge: it's your baby, and you're the host. And don't fuck it up or my next show will be that gladiator-style one with me feeding you to the lions." He slurped some more coffee as he pointed toward the door. "Now go."

"Oh, my God," her best friend Gisele Hornsby said as she took a sip of her wine. They'd gone to their favorite wine bar after work to discuss details of Sophie's new assignment. "This is like your dream. Like your dream of dreams. Like if someone asked you what your impossible-to-attain fantasy job would be, this would be it."

"I know. I keep pinching myself to be sure I'm not just sleeping."

"So what're you going to do?"

"With the sky being the limit, it's awfully hard to narrow it down to something more specific. I feel like I've been given a chance to eat the finest meal I've ever had yet only get one stab at it—do I go for the sumptuous lobster thermidor or the potentially lethal Japanese puffer fish?"

Gisele held up her finger. "I think I can solve your problem. See, I was about to ask for some time off to go visit Tomasso." She'd recently fallen in love with Tomasso Romeo, a member of the Romeo family, which had run the world-famous Italian vineyard *Cantine dei Marchesi Romeo* for centuries. He'd been living in Manhattan under her roof while on a woodworking apprenticeship and had recently returned home. She'd been pining for him badly. "Why don't you take the show to Chianti? Do a big thing with the

Romeo family. Everyone knows Romeo wines, but does everyone know about the opulent lifestyle that comes with being a Romeo? And don't you think your audience—primarily women—would swoon madly for the Romeo men? One more handsome than the next?"

Justin Magruder, Sophie's long-time production assistant, piped in. "Now you're speaking my language. Hot Italian men. Sign me up."

The women laughed. "Italy, huh?" Sophie crossed her arms and rested her hand on her chin in thought. "I could combine this with a search for my Italian roots. And my love of wine, and, well, my love of men, Italian or otherwise."

Justin fist-bumped her. "I'm with you, sister."

"Plus, I mean, all the biggest celebs hang there. George Clooney. Didn't Tom Cruise have one of his weddings there? Beyoncé, she's always on a damned yacht somewhere in Italy."

"You thinking what I'm thinking?" Gisele said, her blue eyes sparkling. She lifted her brow and tucked her long, wavy, blond hair behind her ears.

"Road trip to Tuscany?" Justin said as he flagged the waiter down and ordered a bottle of prosecco.

When the waiter brought back the bottle and uncorked it with a pop, Justin stood.

"This calls for a toast." He lifted his glass and held it to Sophie and Gisele's. "Here's to the best damned team *Gotcha* ever had and is now going to lose to the big leagues." He waved his fingers. "Sayonara, *Gotcha*. And here's hoping we are drowning in the best wine and the best men Italy has to offer."

"Sorry, dude, I've already found my guy," Gisele said

with a grin.

"Fine, then maybe share some of that football team of a family with us. Sophie and I are looking for some Romeo man meat. Amiright, Soph?"

She laughed. "One thing at a time. I want to do this right. Job first, and with any luck, the wine and men will follow."

Chapter Two

LORENZO Romeo was drop-dead gorgeous. And that was saying something coming from the oh-so-handsome Romeo family, in which each of the seven siblings was better looking than the last. For Lorenzo, though, something must have clicked when they put him together, and the media loved to compare him to the ancient Roman god Apollo. It pissed him off. Not that he didn't want to be put on par with higher beings. After all, that was a flattering comparison. But he was sick of being viewed as the family pretty boy and used as such to promote the world-famous wines that came from his family vineyard.

Why couldn't the wines simply sell themselves? Why couldn't they emphasize his brains, not his looks? He knew it sounded sort of silly to feel objectified. It's not as if he was some female supermodel whose job was to make whatever she wore look good. Nevertheless, he was just a family member who was forced to be the face of Romeo wines because he looked so damned good. To him that seemed demeaning.

His five brothers called him a whiny pussy and said he needed to buck up. His sister and mother only laughed and hugged him and told him he was overreacting. And perhaps for this reason, Lorenzo often seemed a bit too defensive and truly relished one-upping his siblings. In fact, he took great pleasure in the conquest. Whether it involved a woman—and he was notorious for his propensity to have his fleeting way with a steady stream of mostly interchangeable women—or business, he was all about setting his sights on his goal and achieving it. Even more so when it meant winning money, which was why he was practically doing a happy dance as his brother Tomasso peeled from a stack of hundred Euro bills, placing them one by one into the palm of Lorenzo's hand.

"Seven, eight"—Tomasso ran his fingers through his thick, wavy black hair and looked up at his brother and glared, his lips pursed—"nine, and ten." With emphasis, he slapped the final bill down. "Take your money, you greedy bastard."

Lorenzo held up his hands. "Greedy? I won the bet fair and square." He grinned, his warm brown eyes sparkling with glee. "I can't help it you couldn't keep your dick in your pants for twenty seconds."

Tomasso shrugged. "Dude, I fought the good fight. But it was worth it because I ultimately came out the winner while you're the one who still has to grovel for a little snatch when you're desperate." He grinned at his brother.

"Spare me," Lorenzo said with a scowl. "I've never begged for a piece of anything a day in my life. Besides, the last thing I'd want is to be tied down to one woman." He grimaced as he tucked a hank of his thick, black hair behind his ear. "Ugh. That would suck."

Tomasso arched a brow. "Try it, you might like it. Intimacy makes the sex even better."

Lorenzo shook his head. "Thanks, I'm good with

incredible sex with any woman I want whenever I want. Can't see ever wanting to narrow my options down when the sky's my limit. I'll leave that to suckers like you." He playfully punched his brother, then pulled out his wallet and stuffed the cash into it. He'd made his brother pay him in bills rather than simply doing a bank transfer—it gave him the opportunity to gloat.

"Suckers, eh?"

"Looks like a duck, walks like a duck, quacks like one."

"So you're an avowed bachelor, then? Never going to settle down?"

"You do know what they say about me," Lorenzo said, a sly grin lifting one side of his mouth.

Tomasso shook his head. "Yeah, yeah. We've all heard it a million times before." He held up his hands and moved his fingers like they were puppets talking. "'Lorenzo put the *roam* in Romeo, blah blah blah, yak yak yak.' Which is actually sort of stupid anyhow because Romeo isn't even spelled the same."

"It's the idea behind it. I like to diversify my options. After all, when you're used to eating gourmet meals every day, why in the world would you ever choose to settle for old, stale leftovers."

Tomasso's eyes opened wide. "My, my, my. You might be slightly older than I am, but you're certainly not wiser. If you think settling down means the sex is worse, you have much to learn. I can assure you I've never had better sex in my life."

Lorenzo opened his mouth to speak yet decided against it.

"What?" Tomasso said.

His brother shrugged. "Oh, nothing. It's just that you

clearly have lived a sheltered life, is all."

"Try it, you might like it."

"God, no." Lorenzo shuddered. "As long as I have blood coursing through my veins, I won't settle down. Variety, my boy, is the spice of life. Besides, commitment gets, well, messy. I don't do messy and I don't do commitment."

"You're certain of that?"

"Sure as the sun will rise in the morning."

"Then why don't you put your money where your mouth is?" Tomasso pointed to the wallet still in his brother's hand.

"What? This?" Lorenzo said, holding the wallet up and opening the section filled with fresh Euros.

Tomasso nodded. "Uh, yeah. You're so sure of yourself and your freedom from the shackles of love. Why not double down on the wager? I paid you a thousand Euros for my arrogance. I say you have to pay me twice that if you can't prove me wrong."

"And how do I prove you wrong but for remaining single?" He laughed. "Do I pay you on my deathbed?"

"Nice try," Tomasso said. "Let's give you the advantage. I'll let you have an entire year. It's a sure bet for you, isn't it? You have to remain single for a year."

"And by single, you mean I can continue to fuck women as long as I don't settle down with any of them?"

"Like I said, this is a sure bet for you. You can graze to your heart's content. At least I had to stay celibate. I'm not even putting those conditions on the bet. Be my guest, go to town, gorge yourself on the buffet of pulchritudinous females. Enjoy your shallow existence, and cash out. On top of it, you get to kick my ass again, which I know is all you need to say yes."

"What's in it for you, then?"

Tomasso shrugged. "Let's just say I've walked in your shoes. And I learned the hard way that never is an awfully long time." He grinned. "Shake on it?"

"Hell yeah," Lorenzo said, thrusting his hand out. "This is going to be the easiest money I've yet to make off you."

His brother lifted an eyebrow. "We'll see, Lorenzo. We'll see."

Chapter Three

SOPHIE rested her chin on Gisele's shoulder as they talked to Tomasso on FaceTime. "You sure this is going to be okay with your family? I mean, I know it's intrusive to show up with a crew and cameras and microphones. Not everyone is keen on sharing their private lives."

Tomasso smiled. "Soph, this is going to be awesome. Seriously I can't wait. Although I have to admit to being selfish since I want to get my girl out here."

Gisele blew a kiss to the screen. "Me too! We're going to have so much fun! We're bringing Justin too. If you can line up some incredibly handsome Italian man for him, go for it. And surely you can find someone for Sophie."

"Oh, I've got someone in mind, all right," he said. "I think it'll be a great match."

Sophie frowned a bit. "You guys! I don't want to be like the pathetic friend you have to find a date for; however, if there's someone who might be fun to do something with, I could possibly be persuaded."

"Not to worry, Soph. I've been thinking long and hard about this. We'll find the right guy for you to make sure that your Italian working holiday is truly memorable."

Sophie clasped her hands together. "I'm just excited for this whole opportunity. It's my chance to shine, so I'm going to have my hand in even the most minute details to make sure it all goes perfectly."

"And anything I can do to help out, let me know. I'm going to assign my brother Lorenzo to remain at your side. Anything you need, he will be right there to be sure it is done without question. I'll, of course, be around as well, but I have a feeling Gisele and I are going to be busy…"

"La-la-la-la," Sophie said, plugging her ears. "I'm going to stay out of this part of the discussion because it is so not my business."

Gisele laughed. "Wait till you're in the same boat. You'll be talking about it to everyone who will listen."

"Honestly, I'm sure this production is going to eat up my time. I'll be lucky if I have a minute to breathe, let alone develop a relationship with a man. Besides, not a lot of men tend to stick around for me."

"Don't sell yourself short," Gisele said.

"Let's just say I have low expectations."

"Maybe you'll find them elevated in Italia," Tomasso said.

"I'll be happy if this show goes off without a hitch. Anything else will be icing on the cake."

"Speaking of sweet things, I can't wait to see you, Tomasso! Stay out of trouble till I get there."

"Does that mean I can get into trouble once you arrive?"

"As long as it involves me." She winked at him.

"Okay, folks, enough with the treacle. All this sweet, gooey talk is going to give me blood sugar problems. Which reminds me—it's time for my daily wine infusion. See you soon, Tomasso!"

It was Sunday afternoon and the entire Romeo family was gathered for lunch. An early spring had emerged from the somnolent winter doldrums that had held Chianti in its grip for months. The Romeos didn't mind the quietude that came with the off-season after the grapes and olives had all been harvested. During the winter months, they could relax for a little bit while planning for the next season. With the weather turning warmer, though, their thoughts turned to planting, and discussion at Sunday lunch inevitably steered toward plans for the Romeo family wines.

Alessandro tapped his wineglass with his knife to get everyone's attention. "For those of you who weren't in on this discussion, I wanted to let you all know the details about the film crew that arrives this week."

"Film crew?" Lorenzo said.

Sandro shot him a look. "Yes. Film crew. We discussed this last Sunday at lunch. Parker's sister's boss is bringing her show here. Featuring Romeo wines, the family, the property, the whole thing." Parker was Gisele's brother, who'd fallen for Sandro and Lorenzo's sister Valentina and was staying with the family for a while so they could spend more time together.

Lorenzo squinted at him. "Um, no one told me this. For that matter, I wasn't even here for lunch last week."

Sandro waved his hand. "We'll get you up to speed now, considering you're going to be the point man for them."

Lorenzo's eyes widened. "I'm sorry. What the hell does that mean?"

"Well, of course, you're the go-to guy for them. That's your job. You're the public face of Romeo wines, which means you'll be the one they deal with. Everything they do while here will be routed through you. And you'll be sitting for interviews with her as well."

"For a bunch of Americans who are going to treat us like some sort of anthropology experiment, observing the strange foreigners from high atop her ivory tower." He made air quotes with his fingers. "'See what the rich Italians do all day!' Worse yet, they'll be like the mean boys holding a magnifying glass up to ants, trying to burn them with the intense focus of light."

Sandro laughed. "Don't you think you're getting a little melodramatic? They're only coming to film us to show their viewers what a magnificent home we have and what wonderful people the Romeos are." He gave a wink to his family. "And when they do that, our wines will fly off the shelves faster than ever back in the States. That's why we're fronting you as the Romeo Americans will grow to love: the face of Lorenzo Romeo sells wine."

"But—"

"But nothing," Sandro said. "We all have a role to play here and this is yours."

"So you're telling me some nosey American television program is coming here to intrude on our privacy and worse, still, I'm the one who has to be a shill for all of the Romeos while they're here?" He shook his head. "Uh-uh. No way. I'm not going to do it. You should have consulted with me before you made these plans and unilaterally decided what I was going to do as part of my job."

Sandro squinted at his brother. "Wait a minute. You seriously think you have a say in this?"

Lorenzo nodded to his mother. "Mamma, be on my side here."

His mother, Fabiana, whose beauty shone through her seventy-some-odd years of age, with graying short hair and loving brown eyes, crossed her arms. "Lorenzo. *Caro*," she said. *Dear.* "Please, let's all get along and enjoy this lovely *pranzo*. After all, you've not been here for lunch in weeks. Can't you simply trust it will all work out fine?"

Alessandro leaned in to whisper in Lorenzo's ear. "What's the matter—you can't defend yourself even at this late age? I thought you abandoned crying for your mamma's support back when you were a kid."

"Watch it, Sandro. I'm not above communicating with these." He held up his fists.

Fabiana stood up and planted herself between her sons, arms extended to keep them apart. "*Ragazzi! Basta!*"

Lorenzo glared. He hated when his mother called them children. The fact was, once again his family made presumptions about his time and interests without even consulting with him and he was so over it. He wasn't behaving childishly. Rather he was standing up for his rights.

"Mamma, this is not your concern."

She furled her brows and lifted her hand to wag her finger at him. "Don't you tell me this is not my business," she said. "You come in and create havoc during my favorite meal of the week. Well, then, even if it wasn't my business, you've made it so. This is my company as well, and I will not have you behaving badly as a representative of this business, which has been well-represented by Romeos for hundreds upon hundreds of years." She put her arms down and turned to face Lorenzo. "Ever since your father died, we have pooled our efforts to keep Romeo wines afloat. Every one of us comes to the table with particular skills. And like it or not, yours happen to include your handsome good looks."

She squeezed his chin between her fingers as if displaying a particularly attractive piece of fruit. Lorenzo winced. She continued her tirade. "If you don't like it, we'll discuss that at a later date. For now, you will be the perfect host, the perfect Sherpa to guide our guests as they film a lovely piece of programming that will help us sell our product. It will drive tourists to our beautiful headquarters, as well as make me happy that we are a well-oiled machine that runs without problems. If you want to go to your room and scream into a pillow about how unfair it is that you happen to be particularly handsome and got stuck being the face of Romeo wines, well, be my guest. If you want a punching bag where you can lash out on your horrible lot in life, I'm sure we can find one for you. But I do not want to hear of one moment in which you aren't the quintessential host to our guests. Not one."

She dusted off her hands as if she'd had a tough day working in the fields. "Now, I expect you to sit down and eat this meal I've fixed for you and I want to see a smile on your face while you're doing it. Is that clear?"

Around the table, the siblings and significant others snickered quietly after holding their mouths silent for a minute.

"And none of you will say a thing, either." She pointed around the table. "Not another word. Now *mangiamo*. Let's eat."

She extended her arm to show Lorenzo where to sit, and again for Sandro as if they didn't already know where they were supposed to be already seated.

Lorenzo knew that in this Italian family, what Mamma wanted, Mamma got. So, for now, he could only stew silently over this decision. In his head, though, it wasn't over yet. Not by a long shot. He'd get in his digs one way or another.

Chapter Four

SOPHIE didn't know which was more treacherous—driving on basically zero sleep in pummeling rain on the Italian *superstrada* with tractor trailers barreling down on her (and the drivers flashing their lights and honking those scary loud horns because, well, she was after all a beautiful woman driving a car in Italy. What else would a man do?). Or driving on perilously twisty mountainous roads as they approached their Tuscan destination, with speed demons on Italian motorcycles whipping around her at every hairpin turn in the road.

"Whose brilliant idea was it to fly into Milan and drive to Chianti?" Gisele moaned as she held her hands to her stomach. She was a bit green around the gills from a bad bout of carsickness.

"How was I supposed to know it would be the drive from hell?" Sophie said. "I figured we'd get to have a nice, leisurely road trip through the Italian countryside, stop and picnic, take in the local color. The flights were cheaper into Milan instead of Florence. I thought I'd save some money and put it toward something else on the production end of things. I was just being a responsible producer."

"I think that's the equivalent of flying into the airport in Boston when your destination is Philadelphia." Justin cupped his hands over his mouth from the back seat to shout so he could be heard over the sound of torrential rain beating down on the roof of the rental car.

They'd flown to Italy ahead of the film crew to have some time to scout things out in person. Sophie had been plunged headlong into research for the past several weeks, learning all she could about Romeo wines and the Romeo family so she could be as knowledgeable as possible beforehand. She'd scoured YouTube for videos people had posted of their vacation tours of the Romeo estate, anything that would help her feel like she had a good handle on her subject.

Through tabloid stories she'd even caught up on some of the more lurid details about certain Romeos' comings and goings: who dated whom, who was engaged, who had issues with crazy ex-girlfriends, and the like. It was kind of fun doing that type of delving. She'd become particularly skillful at it with her previous show, and it seemed second nature to her now. Only this time, she was going to have to remember her guests weren't appearing on her show to basically be humiliated for their boneheaded actions but rather for their chosen lot in life.

"Don't you think you're exaggerating a bit?" She clutched the steering wheel in a death grip. The rain had been so intense, the windshield wipers were doing double-time and she still had a hard time maintaining visibility. On top of that, fog enveloped them at every turn into a low point between the mountains. At one point Sophie had zero visibility with no place to pull over to wait it out. She wasn't a religious girl by any stretch yet felt like a few Hail Marys might hold them in good stead.

"I feel confident that by the time we arrive at *Cantine*

Marchesi Romeo, the sun will be shining, the birds will be singing, and there will be copious amounts of red wine at the ready to settle my nerves a bit."

Justin laughed and Gisele moaned. "I'm gonna need a huge bottle of Pepto Bismol and a warm bed."

"Something tells me that by the time you see Tomasso, you'll forget all about your aching belly and we'll be able to forget about your bellyaching." She turned her head and winked at Justin right as a large truck drove past, splashing water onto the windshield and again temporarily rendering visibility to nil. "Although more than likely we'll be stuck listening to them moanin' and groanin' at that point, which is equally as bad."

"I dunno, Soph," Justin said. "I took a look at their digs online, and I'm pretty sure there will be plenty of distance between rooms to insulate us from hearing those two go at it." He and Sophie laughed.

"You guys are having fun at my expense and if you're not careful, I might just throw up all over the car!"

"Now *that* we don't need. I'm afraid we'll have to leave Gisele on the side of the road if she's going to make this drive any more unpleasant. You with me Justin?" She did a backward high five over the driver's seat.

"Then maybe I should keep from introducing you to Tomasso's brothers, so neither of you can get in on a little action while we're there."

"Well. That would certainly show me." Justin frowned. "Except I already did my due diligence and I know he doesn't have any gay brothers. I'm out of luck with the Romeo clan as it is."

"And I think most of the rest of them are claimed, am I right? That leaves me little chance for anything much anyhow, so I'll take my chances on some stray man I might encounter while here."

They all laughed and as they crested one of those Tuscan hills, saw a brilliant double rainbow hovering over a beautiful Italian villa off in the distance as the rain began to taper off and the sun peeked out from behind the leaden sky.

"Well, would you look at that?" Sophie pointed toward the rainbow, brilliant against the bluing background.

"That megahouse or the crazy-looking sky?" Justin said.

"It's hard to imagine which one is more impressive, isn't it?" It was hard to see details of the place, but high atop the hill stood an imposing yellow *palazzo*, and she knew from her research right away this was their destination. "I think we'll feel pretty much at home—"

Just then a *motocicletta* sped past her and cut her off, causing her to slam on her brakes, the tale of her car fishtailing. Sophie instinctually extended her arm out in front of Gisele next to her as if that would preclude her from going through the windshield in an accident.

"Jesus," she shouted, immediately shoving her middle finger in front of the windshield and holding it there as the guy whizzed past her, flipping her the bird as well. "What a dick! Here I am minding my business, enjoying the scenery, and this jerk tries to kill us. Boy, I'd love to give him a piece of my mind."

"Well, don't worry about him. In a few minutes, we'll be up there." Gisele pointed toward the massive manor home they'd passed in the distance. "We won't have to bother with that idiot ever again."

Sophie smiled. "You know? You're right. We are

smack-dab in the center of heaven right now. Just like I predicted, the sun is coming out and the weather is turning glorious. And we are going to have the time of our lives. I'm not going to let some selfish road hog kill my buzz. After all, I'll never see him again anyhow."

Chapter Five

LORENZO drove like a bat out of hell to get back to the house in time. He'd been duly warned by his mother, and one person he never crossed was Fabiana Romeo. It wasn't as if she was going to give him a spanking or put him in a time-out, but he had a particular soft spot for his mamma ever since his papà died when he was younger.

Back then, each of the Romeo kids handled the loss of their father differently. Some pretended it hadn't happened, as much as that was possible. Some hunkered down and became serious—Sandro chief amongst them, which had always bummed Lorenzo out. Up until that time, the two had been thick as thieves, and together they had pushed the boundaries established by their parents in order to carve independence into their own teenage lives. They got into harmless trouble, wrecking an *Ape*—a sort of dwarfed, three-wheeled truck used to haul equipment on the property—for instance, and mercilessly teasing their sister Valentina, occasionally even sneaking off to the village of Santa Romeo to meet up with girls late at night when they were supposed to be home in bed. Yet when his papà passed, things naturally changed overnight and Sandro became instantly distant and no longer interested in boyish pursuits.

Because Sandro had taken on the role of trying to replace their father, it only made sense for Lorenzo to bear the mantle of tending to his heartbroken mother. And he had quite the knack for it. His mother was crestfallen without her *marito*, and Lorenzo spent his waking hours comforting her broken heart.

He could remember sitting with her, his arm snuggled over her shoulder, as she wailed and sobbed and slept and started the cycle over again. For months Lorenzo stayed by her side, consoling her, cajoling her, doing whatever he could to help her cope in her time of darkness. It was something he tucked away subconsciously, the lesson that loving so deeply could only lead to pain and hurt. Better not to love at all than to love and lose. This he knew from firsthand experience to be true.

Of course a byproduct of being his mother's keeper meant that even now, he never wanted to disappoint her. So when Fabiana told him to be at the house in time for their guests to arrive, he was going to honor her demands even if he truly wanted those guests to be on the next flight back to the States.

He pulled into one of the outbuildings that housed the myriad farm equipment used at the vineyard, taking some time to towel down his beloved gloss-black Ducati. Of course it didn't need to be dried off but it was, after all, the closest he'd ever come to caring for a baby, and he wanted to make sure his beloved charge was supremely well-maintained. Glancing at his Breitling watch, he realized he was late and took off at a rapid clip to get into the house in time.

Still dripping wet, he raced up a set of wide marble steps that were flanked by two flower-filled large urns. He skidded across the marble terrace, slammed open the back door, raced down the hallway past the kitchen, remembering only as he made it to the grand hallway—a museum-like area of the palazzo that was filled with priceless paintings, busts, and statuary—that he'd forgotten to leave his helmet back with the motorcycle. Too late. There stood Fabiana, who threw him a look that could curl straight hair.

With both hands, he lifted his helmet off his head, muttering apologies to his mamma right as she made introductions.

"And finally we have my son Lorenzo, who promised he would be here on time to greet you all. I apologize for his lack of manners."

"Mamma, I'd have been here on time, but there was a carload of tourists with some *pazzo* woman driving like a ninety-year-old nonna. I couldn't get past her for like thirty minutes and it was killing me. God, I wish these tourists would leave the driving to those who live here."

His mother glared. "I'm sure the woman wasn't crazy and was simply driving carefully in the rain. At any rate, as I was saying, Sophie, I'd like you to meet my son, impatient Lorenzo, who I promise, now that he's here, will be at your side during your stay, ready and willing to meet your every need."

At last, Lorenzo looked over and noticed the very head of cascading dark hair he'd glimpsed through the rainy car window only half an hour ago, and his glaring brown eyes met her deep chestnut ones as recognition washed over them both.

"You?" he said in an accusing voice, squinting at her.

"You?" She glared. "With hospitality like we've seen

from you to this point, well, I'd hate to see you at your worst."

Sophie couldn't believe the dripping wet Adonis standing before her. Because, let's be real, even if he was a jerk, he was, without a doubt, a Roman godlike version of a jerk, which would be in keeping with tradition. After all, plenty of Roman gods were kind of dicks, both to each other and to regular, everyday people. So this would come as no surprise. Besides, weren't the hottest guys always the ones with gargantuan egos who thought they were something special?

She'd show him special. If she weren't so tangled up in this commitment to take on the Romeos at this point, she'd catch the first flight out of here and show him how much they would lose in publicity by not having her show here. That wasn't an option and she was stuck, although she didn't have to like it.

She tried not to stare at him as he stood there, a puddle forming around his black leather-booted feet, a look of defiance in his chiseled cheeks and deep-set brown eyes. She had to admit the sexy beard scruff worked well on him, and despite his leather jacket and skintight black jeans being soaked through, his enviable wavy black hair was spared the deluge and looked damned good. As in please-sir-can-I-run-my-fingers-through-it-and-maybe-even-lather-it-up-with-shampoo-when-we-take-a-shower-after-having-frenzied-makeup-sex good.

But hold on one cotton-picking minute—how did she get from wanting to slug this guy to that errant thought? She wasn't even a believer in makeup sex. Though if she thought about it, it was her family legacy. Her mother and father would have knock-down, drag-out fights about stupid things that would end with them banging the headboard in their small Long Island rambler so distractingly loud, you simply couldn't avoid hearing them, try as you might. Even if she turned up the volume on whatever she was watching on the Cartoon Network, it didn't matter. She never understood how you could go from being infuriated with someone to the degree of intimacy commensurate with making love. She needed a long, slow cool-down period before any such "skintimacy" could happen.

That said, if she were to get incredibly irate with a man—like, say, a hot, sexy, Italian man, one whose full lips looked like they could work magic all over her body, dammit—she could see it being with this one. What was his name again? Lorenzo. Lorenzo who had quite the haughty attitude, unfortunately.

Oh well, it was better she didn't have some instant hots for the guy, because, after all, it would be highly unprofessional to even contemplate knocking boots with him. Nevertheless, she decided to tuck a few thoughts of him away in her brain for when she had to resort to her battery-operated boyfriend to do the trick. Oh, yeah. Once she got past this guy's bad attitude, thoughts of a hard, wet, fiery, and passionate Lorenzo Romeo might have to suffice at bedtime after she settled into her private room for the night.

Chapter Six

"MAMMA, if you'll excuse me, perhaps Tomasso can show your guests around. I need to shower and change out of these wet clothes." With that, Lorenzo kissed his mother on either cheek and turned and left the room, leaving her to shake her head in dismay.

"Again, Sophie, Gisele, Justin." Fabiana nodded at the three. "Please accept my apologies for Lorenzo's bad behavior. Trust me, I will have words with him. In the meantime, Tomasso, perhaps you can give the tour and help our guests get settled into their rooms before dinner."

Once she'd departed, Tomasso rolled his eyes. "I don't know what has gotten into my brother, but I hope you'll take it with a grain of salt. Believe me, the rest of my family will more than make up for his little temper tantrum."

Gisele, who'd barely let go of Tomasso since their arrival, pulled him toward her for about their hundredth kiss in the past half hour. "Don't worry. He's all but forgotten," she said after she broke the kiss. "Now let's do the quickie tour because I haven't seen you in weeks." She gave him a wink and as if on cue, both Sophie and Justin stuck their fingers down their throats.

"Don't they just make you want to puke?" Justin elbowed Sophie in the ribs.

"Or find someone I can do that with." Sophie frowned. For some reason, she could only picture herself doing that with that surly Lorenzo, and the more he lingered in her mind, the more she was determined to make good and sure that never, ever happened.

"And now, friends, let's give you the grand tour. After that, everyone can get settled in and unpacked before dinnertime."

They strolled through the grand hallway as Tomasso talked about some of the artwork on display as Sophie stood there, wide-eyed. For a girl who grew up in decidedly working-class suburbia, this place was off the rails in a good way. That people lived like this was truly hard to imagine.

He pointed to a painting by Renaissance painter Titian, another by Raphael. "You caught these at a good time between loans," Tomasso said.

"Loans?"

"Yes, often we let museums all over the world borrow the art that is housed here. What is art if not to share and be enjoyed by as many as possible?"

It was like she was in a private museum. And to think, on top of it all, they had excellent wine here as well. Perhaps she'd died and gone to heaven. Even on their arrival at the palazzo, they'd been greeted by a gorgeous garden in front, with a massive sandstone basin that looked like a bathtub for giants. Like who has that in their yard? Not only was it the Romeos' home, it was their *palace*.

At first, she stood there admiring the buttery-yellow building, taking it all in. A double-ramp staircase led to the main level of the house, fronted by a glorious open-air loggia with statues of gods and goddesses scattered about.

Because, well, who doesn't have statues of mythological characters on the front porch?

Tomasso led them out onto another porch. If you could call it that.

"This is called the *Dell'orologio*," he said. "Which means clock's terrace. And don't ask me why. I should know that but whatever." They laughed.

Sophie leaned on the stone railing of the terrace and stared at the spectacular view: before her as far as she could see, hills and valleys lined with neatly manicured row upon row of cultivated grapevines were interspersed amongst groves of olive trees and wooded forests. In the distance, was a beautiful contemporary structure that integrated so well with the surrounding natural beauty it was almost hard to distinguish it.

"What is that place?" She pointed toward it.

"That"—he nodded in the direction of the building— "is the brainchild of my father, which he sadly never saw to fruition. Alessandro picked up where his dream died, and he saw to it that the headquarters of Romeo wines became a reality. It's even more spectacular than I think our father could have imagined."

The building appeared low on the horizon, built into the land as if emerging from the earth.

"The plan was to build a stunning structure that would become a destination unto itself while maintaining the integrity of the Tuscan countryside," he said. "Which means much of the building is below ground. We also chose to keep it as green as possible, primarily using local materials. It is truly a work of art on so many levels."

"It blends with the terrain as well as the vineyards and olive groves," Sophie said, clucking her approval. "Most impressive." She'd pulled out a notebook from her purse and started to take notes, paying attention to where the sun was tracking across the building. It would help her crew figure out the ideal time to capture the exterior shots and make the building look its best.

He led them down a flight of marble steps, along a flagstone path, and into a garden. The fragrance of roses hung heavily in the air, the heavy rains having amplified the intensity of the aroma. They wandered through a maze of manicured hedges amidst splashes of color, surrounded by a riot of spring flowers in bloom.

Sophie turned to see the most resplendent water fountain: a nearly life-sized burnished statue depicting Bacchus, who, if she recalled correctly, was all about enjoying the bounty of the grape. She nodded at the statue. "That dude is my hero."

Tomasso laughed. "Fun fact: that was a gift from Sophia Loren to my father. They were part of a mutual admiration society."

"Sophia Loren—my namesake! My Italian mamma named me after her. She thought Sophia Loren hung the moon. Though I don't think my mother would have appreciated her giving my father special gifts like this. At least while they were married."

"I think this is kind of like giving someone a leg lamp," Justin said with a laugh.

Gisele high-fived him for alluding to that tacky lamp from the movie *A Christmas Story*. "'*Fragile*, it must be Italian,'" they said in unison and laughed while Tomasso stared at them with a blank look on his face. "Never mind, babe. It's a location joke. I'll tell you about it later."

Tomasso looked at his watch. "I'm glad you

mentioned later because it's getting late and I need to show you to your rooms and give you a chance to rest before dinner. I can assure you Mamma plans to impress you with her cooking prowess tonight. Please do come to dinner with an appetite."

Sophie rubbed her stomach. "I'm all in. And if you throw in a few glasses of red wine I'll be forever at your mercy."

"I think the only mercy you'll need to beg for is from that hottie brother of Tomasso's," Justin said, winking at her.

Sophie let out a growl of disgust. "I'd no sooner apologize to him than ask him on a date."

Tomasso cocked an eyebrow. "My brother doesn't date anyhow, so you're safe. He's all about spreading himself thin if you know what I mean. He's what we call a *figo*, a guy who can always get laid."

"Yet one more reason to avoid that man even if I am stuck with him while we shoot this show." She looked at Tomasso and wrinkled her nose. "Sorry, don't mean to be rude about your brother."

"No worries—I'm with you on that. But I think you'll figure him out. Lorenzo's a straight-up guy, however sometimes his bark is way worse than his bite."

Justin made a purring sound. "I'd like to try his bite just for fun."

"Justin," Sophie and Gisele said in unison. "Down, boy."

They all laughed as Tomasso led them back to the house toward their respective accommodations.

Chapter Seven

SOPHIE had never stayed at the Ritz, nor the Four Seasons for that matter, but she figured the guest accommodations here would have made a room from both those places look like an outhouse on the side of a remote country road. She was already worried about returning home and leaving behind the sumptuous luxury of the world's most perfect bedroom.

After Tomasso had shown them each their rooms, oddly scattered down three different halls —with Gisele's room right across from Tomasso's, the better for late-night visits, no doubt—Sophie took a minute to soak in the splendor that was this room. A large window afforded a brilliant view of the breathtaking Chianti countryside. The room had a sitting area with an overstuffed love seat, a large flat-screen television, and a massive bed that must have been custom sized, it was so huge. It seemed a waste of that much mattress space with only one adult snuggled beneath the fluffy down comforter, so soft and welcoming with its seafoam green velvet duvet cover.

They had two hours before they needed to show up at dinner. Sophie took advantage of the time to unpack her suitcase and get herself organized. She set the luggage on top of the sofa and began to sort and organize things, hanging some clothes in the ample closet across from the even more spacious bathroom, which had a sunken tub and one of those showers with nozzles strategically positioned for just about every need. In an ideal world, she'd happily spend an hour in that shower, or better yet take a soak in the tub, but it would take far too much to get ready all over again. She decided to hold off till she could enjoy it.

Yawning, Sophie stretched her arms and eyed the bed with envy. God, how good would that be to lessen the exhaustion from jet lag with a teensy little nap? Everyone says that's a mistake: if you want to adjust your circadian rhythm, you simply tough it out and go to bed at night in the new time zone.

She reached into one of the zippered sections of her suitcase and pulled out her socks and jewelry, placing them in the top dresser drawer. Next she unzipped the other one and extracted her panties and bras, putting them away in the drawer next to it. She noticed a stray battery and fumbled in the suitcase looking for what the battery belonged to when her hand settled on her travel-sized pocket rocket.

"Well, that's embarrassing," she muttered, assuming airport security had a field day rifling through her luggage and finding her vibrator there. No doubt they had a good laugh at her expense. "Thank God they didn't pocket it themselves. I'm gonna need this, especially with that brother of Tomasso's lurking. I can tell that man is going to test my resolve."

Sophie held it up to the light and reinserted the battery, annoyed the TSA couldn't have extended her the courtesy of doing so themselves, and tucked it into her lingerie drawer. She yawned again, eyeing the bed.

"Maybe a quick catnap." She unbuttoned her white silk blouse and draped it over a nearby chair, then unzipped her black leather pencil skirt and shimmied out of it, placing it next to her shirt. She unhooked the front of her bra, kicked off her black leather pumps, and didn't even bother pulling down her thigh-high stockings, figuring she'd have to put them back on in time for dinner anyhow.

She drew back the comforter and slid beneath its welcoming billow, groaning at how perfect it felt. Her mind began replaying the past couple of hours in her head, and like a record with a scratch on it, her thoughts kept getting stuck on that moment when Lorenzo lifted his helmet over his head, his biceps flexing through his thin, black cashmere sweater, his powerful thighs highlighted by the soaking wet jeans clinging to them. And doing little to conceal what he was packing in those pants. She moaned. What a shame circumstances weren't different—otherwise she'd have loved to try to tempt him into a little game of one and done. She wasn't looking for commitment either, and he looked like he might be a lot of fun to spend an hour or two with. As long as he kept his mouth shut. Except to use his tongue as needed.

Argh. That tongue. So far, she'd only been on the receiving end of its worst. She wondered how amazing it could be when he was using it for good. His brother suggested he was a bit of a player. Which meant he was probably quite gifted at servicing a woman's needs. And with lots of experience. Women who migrated toward his type usually made sure to teach men what worked best. It was probably the only good thing about a man with a history of many previous lovers.

She thought about that pocket rocket, mulling whether

that might be the perfect thing to cut the edge off, to enable her to deal with him at dinner without her mind going down that wayward path. The more she contemplated it, the more it seemed to be the smartest option when it came down to it. Finally she went to the dresser, pulled her toy from the drawer, and returned to that heavenly bed, briefly admiring the hand-carved mahogany headboard and noticing the enormous chandelier that hung suspended over part of the bed. She hoped that thing was securely installed so as to not impale her in the middle of the night. It would be a bad headline: *Sleeping Woman Crushed by Light Fixture*. If she was going to die in bed, it damn well better be beneath the weight of a strong, handsome man, not a decorative crystal chandelier.

Sophie snuggled back down again, this time not even bothering to cover herself with the duvet; it would only be in the way. She pulled out the toy, flicked the switch, and heard it come to life. She loved the power of this thing but damn, it could be a bit loud. Good thing she was far away from everyone, alone in this wing of the house. She placed the vibrating head on her nipple, teasing it to a stiff peak, then switched to the other.

Closing her eyes, she fantasized that it was hotheaded Lorenzo Romeo's tongue flicking over the hard tip. She moaned, guiding the toy down her body and slowly pressing it over her panties. As it hit the sweet spot, she moaned again and spread her legs wider, wishful that a man was the one busy pleasuring her and had spread her legs because he needed more room to maneuver.

She continued to pinch her nipples with one hand while she slid the vibrator beneath the edge of her panties, moving it along her already-slick center, pretending it was

Lorenzo's hand slipping beneath her panties. She imagined him pressing his fingers inside of her, pushing deep, and pulling out, learning the rhythm that her body craved. Mimicking the motion he would use, she urged the vibrator deeper as she moved closer to orgasm. The explosion of sensations rapidly diffused as she suppressed a loud moan, imagining that the vibrator buried deep was Lorenzo's hot, hard cock about to release inside her. She came hard, her body trembling as she held the vibrator deep to make the climax last as long as possible.

As she shuddered once more, her body eventually settling down, she almost felt like she could come again as she fantasized about that rogue Romeo—something she'd done only once before on the heels of one orgasm. She decided to keep the pocket rocket inside for another minute to see what would happen, but within seconds, her jet lag caught up with her, and she fell fast asleep.

Chapter Eight

LORENZO wondered if the coast was clear. After showering and changing into dry clothes, he'd resolved that his best strategy was going to be avoidance at all costs. He wondered: was it bad that at the same time he wanted to send that Sophie woman packing, he also wanted to lift her up, wrap her long legs around his hips, and fuck the daylights out of her? Surely that was simply his overactive dick talking. After all, she was a stunningly beautiful woman. What man in his right mind wouldn't want to take her up against the wall? Or have her on her knees, her soft, black hair coiled around his fists as he watched, mesmerized, while her mouth hungrily enveloped his swollen cock.

He was going to have to get into town tonight, where he'd have his pick from a ready stable of women who would gladly satisfy his needs and help erase Sophie whatever-her-name-was from his mind.

He stepped from his room into the hallway but stopped suddenly upon hearing an unfamiliar noise coming from the room across from his. Weird. That room wasn't used by anyone. Maybe the housekeeper had left some sort of cleaning device on.

At the door, he turned the knob and entered.

Whatever it was, he needed to be sure it was shut off. Who knows? It could be a fire hazard or something.

The bigger fire hazard, though, was what he was treated to the minute he opened the door: his cock sprang to life so fast he was going to need a fire extinguisher to put it out. Spread out on the bed, either sound asleep or dead, was none other than that troublemaking American, Sophie, with the most gorgeous set of tits bared for his viewing pleasure.

He was so captivated, he could barely think for a minute, but then he again noticed that buzzing sound and wondered what the hell it was. His eyes scanned her rockin' body, hating to leave those hot tits, yet slowly moving down her narrowed waist to that sheer pair of white panties. She clearly had a talented aesthetician, who'd executed a masterful Brazilian wax on that beautiful snatch of hers. Good Lord, he practically had to stuff his tongue back in his mouth. Hopefully he wasn't drooling. Taking in her long, lusty legs, with those sexy-as-hell black thigh-highs that always made him crazy, he had to catch his breath.

Slowly he approached, still hearing that nagging noise humming. When he moved closer to her body, he could tell it was coming from there. As in *there*. His favorite place in the world: that warm, wet, delectable place that seemed to be made just for his cock.

But crap. This one was so off-limits it was almost unfortunate. Because he suddenly knew precisely what that buzzing sound was—a vibrator. The woman had fallen asleep with a vibrator up her *figa*.

I'll be damned if that's not the hottest fucking thing I have ever seen.

He tried to clear his hormone-addled brain for a minute, to move his thought center back up from his dick to his other head, trying to figure out what the protocol would be under such circumstances. He couldn't imagine it was good for somebody to have a vibrator buzzing up there for a long period of time. Though it wasn't as though he could reach inside and pull it out. Could he? Damn, that was the stuff of fantasies: you happen upon a woman spread wide for you, sound asleep after an amazing orgasm, and you get to slide your fingers inside her slick body to pull out a vibrator. And maybe replace it with something more lifelike. Perhaps she'd fallen asleep without ever achieving one, and she was desperate to come. With his skillful assistance. He groaned, and pressed his hand against his crotch, trying to adjust his dick, which kept getting harder by the minute.

He paced while pondering this. *Well, crap. What to do?* This was almost an enviable problem to have, at least until said woman stirred.

There was a loud gasp.

"You!" she screamed, covering her breasts with her hands. Lorenzo momentarily turned his face away, about as guilty as if he'd been caught with his hand in her wallet. At least that was tamer than getting busted with his hand in her *patata*.

"You!" he said, pointing at her like an idiot. Perhaps he should cover up the evidence of his own arousal, he thought, considering she was suddenly hiding herself from him.

"What the hell are you doing here?" she stammered, before obviously collecting her thoughts. "Oh, my God. What are you doing here?"

"I, uh, uh, uh"—he pointed to her crotch—"I heard a concerning sound out in the hallway. This room is usually vacant. I heard a buzzing sound. I came in here to be sure there wasn't something dangerous happening."

Oh, but there was something seriously dangerous happening here.

If her face hadn't already turned a few shades redder, it did when she glanced down toward her crotch as the buzzing continued.

The two seemed frozen in place. Lorenzo watched a look wash over her face, one of near pain and pleasure all rolled into one as she squeezed her eyes shut and her hips bucked. She let out a soft moan.

Holy fuck. She just came. In front of him. With nothing but a vibrator in her cooch.

This had to be the hottest thing he'd experienced with a woman ever. And he hadn't even touched her.

"Uh, can I be of assistance?" He hoped against hope she'd say yes. Maybe even beg him to join in the fun.

She quickly regained her composure, pulled the comforter over her exposed body, and reached down, evidently removing the offending toy because the buzzing became louder. After she fumbled beneath the blanket a bit more, the sound stopped.

Count this as one of the rare moments in his life when he wanted desperately to cry, so bereft he was that this magical moment had ended. What loomed before him now was likely a massive freak-out from the naked woman in front of him.

Chapter Nine

WELL, fuck. What the hell do you do when you fall asleep with a pocket rocket up the docket, only to have your host-enemy discover you in a state of self-pleasure-slash-passed-out-cold? Sophie tried to imagine if she could even pull up this question on her phone. Surely every question had at this point been asked of Google, but perhaps she would be the one to introduce this one to the world. She couldn't imagine that any woman in the history of the planet had ever found herself quite in this situation.

She looked up at Lorenzo, whose eyes were glazed over with lust, and her eyes trailed down his body to see his cock pressing against his blue jeans in an undeniable outlined proof of sexual desire. As if it wasn't bad enough that she a) fell asleep with a vibrator in her, and b) woke up with a hot but jerky guy hovering over her because of the loud vibrator stuck inside her, but then she c) orgasmed despite herself right there as he watched—the hat trick of sexual humiliation—well now he stood there obviously horny as hell, as she lay there, embarrassed to the nth degree, and it was like the world's most awkward standoff.

Well, crap. What was she to do now?

First off, get him the hell out of here.

"I think you've seen quite enough, don't you? I'll thank

you to leave." She lay there like a cadaver awaiting an autopsy, only able to point toward the door as she remained hidden beneath the comforter, bashful after her unplanned exposure. What a mess. Here she was fantasizing about having sex with the man and whammo—he happens to appear at the most inopportune of times.

He held up his hands.

"Look, I was across the hall in my room. I only opened the door because I was worried there was something wrong in here that could catch fire. How would I have known that the only thing heating up was you?"

If this was some porn flick, no doubt he'd have jumped right in. And she'd have welcomed it with open arms. But shit, not like this was for real! How was she going to face him? That is after he left the room. Here she thought she'd tamp down the sexual energy that had threatened to make dinnertime more stressful, and now she wondered how she was going to be in this man's presence ever again.

"Get. The. Hell. Out. Now." Her voice was stern and unequivocal.

He turned and she watched him skulk out of the room, walking as if he had a two-by-four wedged in his crotch. Normally she'd gladly take credit for the hard-on that was inhibiting his gait, yet under the circumstances, uh, not so much.

Sophie stood, dragging the blanket with her, still covering her naked breasts, and bolted the door shut.

She took a deep breath and released it. There was no choice: she was simply going to have to put on her game face and pretend this never happened. And hope like hell he didn't share with the world what he was privy to in a most unwelcome way.

She was going to have to get online and find a super-silent vibrator to replace this betrayer of a sex toy, dammit.

Lorenzo was in a state of shock. In a million years, never could he imagine the series of events that had unfolded this afternoon. First he was stuck in the driving rain with some idiot *puttana* driving like his hundred-year-old nonna, oblivious that he was being drenched to the bone. Even when he drove right up on her ass, still she ignored him. And she ended up being the very woman he had been racing back to meet, only because his mother would have strung him up if he'd refused.

He could barely stop himself from behaving so coarsely. It wasn't like him to be such a rude person, but he was tired and cold and wet and annoyed and his mood had gotten the better of him. And then this, the most miraculous of things to ever transpire before his eyes. Turns out the bitch wasn't a bitch at all but molto *strafiga*. Smoking hot. With perfect tits that were the perfect size to fit in his large hands. *Mentre ditalino*! While practically fingering herself! *Mio Dio*. He shook his head in amazement. *My God*, indeed.

Well, there was no way he was ready to show his face (and particularly his swollen cock) in the main part of the house quite yet. No longer could he wait to go into the village tonight to seek satisfaction. He was going to have to take care of this himself before he blew a gasket… or something.

He returned to his room and wasted no time stripping off his clothes. Grabbing the lube he kept in his nightstand, he squirted an ample amount into his palm, quickly grabbing his cock and moaning at the pleasurable feel of his fingers clasping around it at last.

It might as well have been her fingers wrapped delicately around it; that's what he was telling himself, anyhow. He wished he was that guy who would have joined right in and assumed she'd be on board with the plans. Maybe bury his face in her *figa*, stroking his tongue along the slick center. He groaned at the idea, pulling harder on his cock, and reaching down to fondle his balls, too.

His preference then would be to flip her over onto her hands and knees and drive his cock into her slickness from behind, *alla pecorina*, sheep-style.

He was lost in his fantasies, balls deep in the woman of his dreams, pounding stroke after punishing stroke deep into her wet pussy as he clutched her shapely ass between his hands. He didn't even hear the door creak open. Or notice the woman approach the bed, her jaw agape, eyes wide, hand quickly covering her mouth.

"Sophie!" Lorenzo said on a loud shout, his eyes squeezed shut, as semen shot from his swollen cock, coating his belly with proof of what she'd done to him.

Chapter Ten

SOPHIE? He called out *her* name while he jacked off? She assumed that meant he'd been fantasizing about her while doing so, which wasn't actually at all offensive. Considering the compromising position she'd found herself in not fifteen minutes ago, she was at least relieved it had turned him on… and a bit disturbed that it was now turning her on even more. Did this mean she had some voyeur fetish she didn't know about? She'd never had a strange man watch her climax before. Putting aside the mortification factor that came with this situation, well, in a dirty way it was kind of hot as hell.

After all, it's not like he was a complete stranger. Well, okay, he had been a rude jerk to her. But Tomasso said Lorenzo could be brusque. And she did at least already know Tomasso. For that matter, she had even pretended she was going to have sex with Tomasso awhile back only to make Gisele jealous and force her to admit she had feelings for the man, in a deranged matchmaker sort of way. So it was almost like a reward for that good deed: here she'd gotten an even hotter version of Tomasso for her efforts. And what else did it get her? Dueling peep shows, evidently. Oy. The whole thing was weird, awkward, and uncomfortable, yet oddly a turn-on.

So did that mean she liked to watch, or be watched? And why, dammit, did she have this unnerving compulsion right this minute to want to straddle his sticky wet belly and slide her rapidly dampening self all over it? Good Lord— was this the hot Italian in her, finally emerging, now that she'd stepped foot in the motherland?

She'd never considered herself to be a prude in bed by any stretch of the imagination. Hell, she'd even had a threesome once in college. She liked to think she dabbled, had a little adventurousness in her. There was something about this man, though, who'd given off the distinct vibe he hated her yet was obviously turned on by what he saw her do. And well, wow—now this.

"*Merda*," Lorenzo said as his shrinking cock slipped from his fist. Shit. "*Porco dio.*"

Sophie knew from hearing Tomasso say this phrase that it was an expression their mother hated—something many Italians might use frequently, although it technically was disrespecting God. As a Catholic, Fabiana wouldn't have any of it. Sophie had even picked up saying it, it was so catchy. Good thing his mother wasn't around to hear it spring forth from his lips. Then again, it was an even better thing that she wasn't around to have seen what happened with her a short while ago in her room. While her son watched. Oh God.

"Um, uh, er." Sophie scrunched her face, lifted her hand, and cupped her fingers, wiggling them in a half-hearted hello.

"Is this some sort of revenge thing?" He wiped his damp hands across his chest and continued to lay there, naked and spread-eagled, looking downright edible, with his broad, smooth chest, cut abs, thick thighs, and oh, never mind. What was it about guys that they had absolutely no embarrassment about their bodies or about what their bodies did (usually) in the privacy of their own home? The man looked like women popped in on him *in flagrante delicto* every day. Caught red-handed. Or red-cocked. Sophie let out a giggle at that. At least her hands weren't involved when he witnessed her. Obviously that vibrator didn't get there by itself, but it seemed it would have been even more embarrassing if she had been in the midst of rubbing one out.

Who was she kidding? Tom-a-to, tom-ah-to.

"I'd like to say I'm sorry, but under the circumstances, I'm not particularly upset that you seem to have evened the score." She shrugged her shoulders.

One side of his mouth lifted into a grin. "Busted."

They stood there in silence for ten seconds.

"Soooo, you rang?" he said.

She winced. "I guess I was coming over to explain what happened and to try to come to some sort of meeting of the minds over how to handle this. Because, well, after all, I'm going to have to work with you and you're going to have to work with me—"

He shook his head. "Don't remind me."

She frowned, and a dead silence again descended on the room. To avoid staring at his cock, which actually seemed like it was trying to ring the bell to start round two, she glanced around the room, which felt manly, in keeping with the man who oozed masculinity. The walls were a smoky gray and the furniture a sleek, contemporary Italian style, completely different from the Renaissance-style that defined her room. This man's room would make a man want to tug up his pants at the thigh, straddle a bar stool, and toke on a Cuban cigar while bragging about his latest sexual conquests. All after a hard day's labor.

Again she giggled. The two of them had knocked out some manual labor, alrighty.

"I'm naked before you and you laugh?" He squinted at her. "This is not good for a man's ego."

"Oh, no, I didn't mean it like that. I just had some thoughts run through my head that made me laugh. It had nothing to do with you. Well, I mean of course it had to do with you even though it wasn't because of you." She pointed at his dick. "I mean that. I wouldn't laugh at that. Trust me on that."

Really? Had she said that?

"You like it?"

Her eyes grew wide. How does one answer such a question? From a technical standpoint, hell to the yeah. She saw how big that thing was when he was about to explode. One thing she learned early on: size matters. So, yeah, she liked it plenty. But she wasn't exactly entitled to have a say in it, technically. After all, he was here doing his business and she accidentally happened upon it. Then again…

She cocked her head at him. "You said 'Sophie.'"

He looked at her, confused. "Huh?"

"You called out my name when you—"

It was his turn to shrug. "I walk in on a strafiga—a beautiful woman—who must have fallen asleep pleasuring herself. Mind you, I'm not sure how you would fall asleep in the middle of that, and that's your business. But you wake, and without even trying, your body shudders in pleasure from a climax right before my eyes. Uh, yeah, after that, and before you cut off my balls for being there, I had to take care of matters myself, *prontissimo.*" He grinned.

"And considering that was the hottest fucking thing I've ever seen, it was you in my mind *quando mi do una sega.* When I gave myself a hand job, I imagined I was fucking you. Doggy style."

Sophie blanched and cleared her throat.

Well. How do you respond to that? Why thank you for getting yourself off to thoughts of having sex with me. Even though we don't exactly know each other. Although in a weird way, we sort of know each other intimately. Ish.

Good Lord, now she knew how Kim Kardashian must feel, thinking of all the boys who masturbated to thoughts of her big, frequently-bared-to-the-world naked ass.

At least Sophie hadn't been in the habit of flaunting what she had in that manner. As long as this remained between the two of them, she could be sure no one else would be looking at her, thinking of doing it doggy style.

"Um, thank you? I guess?"

"Surely you must know that men always think of beautiful women they encounter when they're masturbating."

She arched a brow. "I guess different strokes for different folks?" She laughed at her own joke.

He bent his elbows and clasped his hands behind his head. She could see the hair beneath his armpits, her Achilles heel. Something about that made her want to drag her hands and tongue across his body like a hungry animal. God, she needed to calm the hell down.

"Can I ask you something?" She had to. She needed some reassurance.

He nodded.

She moved her finger slowly back and forth between them. "This," she said, hesitating. "Now that we're even, can we agree to keep this between the two of us? Because I would about die if word ever got out. I mean this is a really important assignment I'm on. I can't screw up. And what happened today, well, not only would that be considered a huge professional screwup, my boss would never let me live it down. In fact, he'd be sure to have it carved on my tombstone. And I'd probably insist on being cremated to avoid that shame. Nevertheless, being a media guy, he'd be sure it was the lede in my obit."

He gave her a look that told her she was speaking part gibberish to him. While his mastery of the English language—even transcending sexual talk—was pretty impressive, clearly some of the colloquialisms escaped him.

"Promise me you won't tell anyone about what happened here. I could lose my job. I know you're not excited that we're here, but, well, we're here. Sorry." She shrugged. "No one warned me about your objections. I'll try to stay out of your way and you can avoid ever mentioning this episode again. Ever."

"*Capisco.* I understand."

She clasped her hands together and, stretching them backward, cracked her knuckles, a nervous habit she'd picked up in grade school and continued to this day. "In that case, I think I'll go try to put my clothes on right-side out." She pointed to the tag hanging off the cami top she'd quickly thrown on in her haste to catch him before he blabbed to the world about her embarrassment. "And I'll pretend I don't know you at dinner." She forced a half-hearted smile.

He nodded as he dragged his hands across his chest, making her envy the hell out of those hands. "*Va bene, bella.* Va bene." It was good. Or at least she hoped it would be.

Chapter Eleven

LORENZO didn't mind one bit that the hot producer sat at the dinner table like a gazelle ready to take a flying leap as soon as a lioness pounced. The fact was, while he couldn't believe his good fortune at witnessing what he had with her today, it still didn't erase that he didn't want her and her crew to invade his privacy and make some sort of entertainment television show about his family's life.

It was weird. And awkward. And meddlesome. And on top of it, everyone was expecting him to yet again play the role of the most handsome of the Romeos. He was completely over that. He simply wanted to be a working Romeo and not the go-to beauty queen of the family. If anything, that mantle should belong to his sister Valentina, not that she'd wear it either. It was strange being judged by your looks. Though if he were honest, he'd acknowledge that his looks had held him in good stead over the years. It took little to no effort for him to land whatever woman he wanted on any given night, for instance. Still, he didn't want to be the family pretty boy. There was much more to him than his superficial good looks.

As he wandered down the corridor on his way to dinner, he hoped he wouldn't run into that woman. He was going to need a little space between them or he was going to be in a semihard state for the next however long she was here.

He arrived at the dinner table in time to see Gisele greet her brother Parker, who'd left New York to join his girlfriend, Tomasso's sister Valentina, months earlier.

"Parks! I'm so happy to see you finally!" Gisele practically jumped into his arms.

"Happy to see me, but happier to see this one." He directed his thumb at Tomasso. "Because I know you've been with him all day and never even went out of your way to find me." He pushed his lip in a fake pout.

Gisele frowned. "So maybe Sophie and Justin and I were just getting our bearings! But we're here! Aren't you excited!"

"You're like a giant exclamation point. I am thrilled to have you here, sis. I think you'll like it."

"I trust Lorenzo made sure that you were comfortable?" their oldest brother Alessandro turned to ask Sophie.

Lorenzo glanced at Sophie in time to see a blush of pink shimmying up her neck to her face. Although she tried to look away, he stared right at her.

"Uh, yes, very at ease."

"You might even say I made sure she was stress free."

She clenched her jaw.

"Well, that's quite a turnaround from earlier this afternoon, Lorenzo. I'm glad you've seen the light," Sandro said.

"If only you knew what I've seen." He arched a brow and grinned.

Sophie's eyes opened wider than seemed natural, which entertained Lorenzo to no end. He was finding it great fun to see her squirm. Yet as soon as she had a chance, she threw him the side-eye, letting him know what she thought about his toying with her like that.

Toying. With her. Which made him think of her battery-operated toy. Which made him rearrange his napkin on his lap so no one could see his pants suddenly growing tighter.

He momentarily closed his eyes and all he could see was her hand on his cock. And all he could hear was her groaning his name. Ever since he'd found her with that toy inside her, he'd wondered what it would be like to be buried deep within her. He would tense, his nerves on edge and his muscles rigid. When he would call out "Sophie," she'd pull him in even deeper, maybe while her tongue mimicked in his mouth what his cock was doing in her pussy. He shook his head. Merda. What the hell was wrong with him? He had to excise her from his brain. She was off-limits.

"Fabiana, this is truly amazing food." Sophie swallowed a bite of the wild boar stew Fabiana had prepared. "Had I known how perfect authentic Italian food would be I would have come back to the homeland sooner."

His mother smiled. "No need to flatter me, dear. I think it's lovely that you've finally come to Italy and I hope we can make it a fantasy holiday for you."

Lorenzo winced. Without a doubt, it started with a bang-up fantasy, that's for sure. More like a banging fantasy. One that continued to loop through his head more than he cared to admit.

"Sandro, I understand your fiancée is Taylor McFarland, the famous model? That must be exciting,"

Sophie said as she took a sip of her wine.

He smiled. "She's amazing. I only wish she could be here all the time. Her career keeps her traveling far too frequently."

"You're going to need to put a *bambino* in her to settle her down," Lorenzo said.

Sophie's head whipped around to glare at him. "How very paternalistic of you. Maybe he could just plant a flag on her and colonize the woman."

Lorenzo mentally ground his teeth as he counted to three before replying. "There's something wrong with getting her pregnant?"

Sophie sputtered. "With getting pregnant? No. With wanting to place handcuffs on your wife or girlfriend or whatever the hell she is to keep her down on the farm? Uh, yeah, I'd say so."

Lorenzo looked at Sandro and said something in rapid-fire Italian then winked at his brother. The two men laughed. Gisele threw Tomasso a searing look that must've kept him from joining in the fun.

"What did he say?" Sophie said to Tomasso, who looked as if he was in the middle of an Inquisition and risked losing a couple of digits if he gave the wrong answer.

"Just a little joke about strong-willed American women," Sandro said.

"Oh, because strong American women are a threat to dominant Italian men?"

Lorenzo caught Justin squinting at Sophie as he dragged his finger across his throat, the international symbol of *shut-the-hell-up*.

"I didn't say that." A look of bemusement danced in Lorenzo's eyes. "It's only that certain women seem to have a need to—"

"*Basta*!" Fabiana clapped her hands. "No disrespecting our guest of honor." She reached over to pat Sophie's other hand.

"Well," Sandro said, saving the conversational lull, "in answer to your suggestion, Lorenzo, we've talked about a timeline, but we're in no hurry. Besides, even if she does have children, she'll still model. Marriage and parenthood don't curse you for all eternity."

Lorenzo frowned yet didn't respond. He knew differently.

"What our guests don't know is that with our brother Lorenzo, here, you've met the last of a dying breed: the avowed bachelor. Never to marry, no matter what." Tomasso gave his brother a mocking two thumbs-up.

Lorenzo took a sip of his wine and smirked back at him.

"How can anyone flat-out say they'll never settle down?" Gisele said. "It seems strange. How do you know? Maybe you'll meet someone tomorrow and all of that will change. If you don't give it a chance, you're missing out."

"I'm happy that settling down works for you. For me, though, it feels like settling, period. And it's of no interest to me. Besides, what if I made the decision to spend the rest of my life until the end of time with one woman, only to find a better one the very next day?"

"Gee, don't do the women of the world any huge favors," Sophie said under her breath as she rolled her eyes.

"I'm serious," he said. "What is the likelihood that you have this one person you are predestined to spend your life with? Hardly a day goes by I don't happen upon a woman I'd like to get to know, and if I were married, I couldn't do that."

"And I'm sure you figure it's far more generous of you to share that manhood of yours with as many women as possible," Sophie said, her eyes going wide as if she immediately regretted saying it the minute it passed her lips.

"Well, would you look at the clock. It's getting late." Tomasso tapped on the face of his watch, yawning and stretching his arm around Gisele's shoulder. "You guys have a lot of work to do tomorrow and I'm sure no one was able to sneak in a nap today. You all must be exhausted."

"I think Sophie here had a good nap. Possibly even the best nap ever." Lorenzo grinned as she threw him the stink-eye.

"Fabiana, your bed is tremendously comfortable. Lorenzo is right. I slept like a baby. Now if you'll excuse me, I think I will take advantage of the chance to get a good night's sleep. *Grazie mille* for your wonderful hospitality."

But Lorenzo was not going to be satisfied letting her have the last word and moments later politely excused himself from the table as well.

Chapter Twelve

SOPHIE didn't know how she escaped from that meal without her house of cards collapsing before her eyes. The sheer arrogance of that man made her absolutely crazy. She wanted nothing more than to shake some sense into him and remind him that it was the twenty-first century and he wasn't put on this earth to give women as many orgasms as possible before he died of too much sex.

She picked up the pace as she walked briskly down one corridor and another toward her room, not even stopping to admire the beautiful works of art scattered around her.

"So let me get this straight," she heard the rich timbre of Lorenzo's voice echo from behind her. "'It's far more generous of you to share that manhood of yours with as many women as possible'?" She stopped and turned to see where he was in time for him to run smack into her.

"Oof!" she said as his chest pressed into hers, which shouldn't have felt as welcoming as it did.

"*Cara*," he said, his hands pausing against her shoulders as he eyed her from top to bottom. "I thought we had an agreement that our little episodes were not to be discussed in mixed company."

"I wasn't discussing that, per se. I was merely remarking on the fact that you seem to be under the impression that you're God's gift to what you would consider the fairer sex and what I could rightly claim as the stronger sex."

He let out a whistle as he shook his head. "You are one piece of work, you know that?"

"Takes one to know one." Did she actually say that? Invoking schoolyard taunt number seventy-two in lieu of a snappier comeback? She glanced down at his hands that were still pressed to her shoulders, perilously close to her breasts, which rose and fell with the increasingly rapid breaths she was taking. Why did he make her so skittish? She was not a woman who let a man get under her skin. Growing up, she learned from watching her parents' volatile relationship that doing so would only lead to tears and heartache, if not sooner, then later.

"Cara, I'm afraid even a strong woman such as yourself couldn't handle even one night with me."

Well, shoot. First off, she wanted to remind him that her name was Sophie, not whoever this Cara chick was he kept referring to. Figures, the guy had slept with so many women he couldn't even keep the names straight with any female he met. Second, she was not one to let a gauntlet be thrown and unanswered. And that was one hell of a gauntlet he left dangling before her.

"What, because of your godlike sexual stamina? Or because of that thing you're packing?" She stole a downward glance at it.

He shook his head, perhaps not expecting her to be that blunt. "My experience is it's best not to go to the deep end if you don't know how to swim."

She glared at him. "And you're suggesting that I'm somehow a rookie? I don't have the resume for a roll in the hay with you?"

He arched his brow and gave her a half smile. "Trust me, cara, you'd need a life preserver to get in deep with me."

"That's good because you'll never be deep in me." She smiled. Score: Sophie one, Lorenzo zero.

"Suit yourself. However if you'd like me to take you under consideration, I can be flexible, and I'm always open to suggestions."

"Thanks, but I don't think you could handle the likes of me."

He shook his hand as if he'd touched something hot. "Oh, cara, I can assure you, there, you're sorely mistaken." He leaned forward, coaxing her chin toward him with his finger. He gently pressed his mouth to hers, subtly stroking his tongue against her lips until she opened hers and they deepened the kiss. It wasn't lost on Sophie as she betrayed her own best intentions that he was likely doing the same since she could feel him grow instantly hard, pressed up to her as he was. She decided to double down, grinding her hips against him till they both moaned.

Lorenzo's fingers skimmed over her ass, along her narrow waist, and ultimately settled on her breasts. Working his strong hands over them, he kneaded and rubbed like a master baker taking care to be gentle yet firm with his bread dough. Meanwhile Sophie's hands trailed down Lorenzo's back, pressing against his perfectly shaped ass so she could feel his hard length against her even more clearly. Wow, that man was packing one hell of banana.

At last, Lorenzo broke the kiss as Sophie let out a moan. "You see, cara, I can handle you with great ease. But this is where it must end, because I want to be abundantly clear about this: I'm not happy that you and your freak show have invaded my family's personal space, and I'm not going to pretend I am. I will put on a smile and fake it in front of my mother because she's my mother. Please, don't expect me to bend over backward to make this easy for you, though, because I won't."

Stunned at his duplicity, Sophie froze for a second before doing the only thing she could think to do under the circumstances. Raising her hand, she slapped him hard across that smug face he was so proud of. She wanted to hit him where it hurt, and clearly that was his Achilles heel.

Dammit, she could kick herself for being such a rube, falling for the oldest trick in the book. Leave it to Lorenzo to use his dick to try to mess with her head. Though that sounded weird if taken literally. Which made her half laugh, trying to imagine him poking at her head with that well-endowed piece of equipment he was packing. Ugh. Like it or not she had to admit she was, for some bizarre reason, profoundly sexually attracted to him. Thank God he had the personality of a battering ram because no way in hell was she ever going to capitulate to any more advances or sneak attacks he might have planned for her. She was a strong woman and knew better than to yield to the likes of Lorenzo Romeo. Sure he had a hot face and a hard cock— he also obviously had an even harder heart, and she knew what cold-hearted men were like, thanks to a lifetime of watching her father disrespect her mother time and again, only to have her ultimately relinquish herself to him.

She turned to retreat to her room to lick her wounded ego, yet as she turned the knob on the door, she glanced over her shoulder at him as he still stared at her, rubbing his cheek against the sting.

"Can I ask you something personal?"

He gave her a "no duh" look. As if they'd not already been a bit personal with one another.

"I'm wondering how you would say doggy style in Italian."

He frowned. "After all of this, you want to know that?"

She shrugged. "Just curious, I guess."

"Alla pecorina. Pecorina means 'sheep.'"

"Wasn't that pecorino cheese we ate after dinner tonight? Now I'll never have that cheese without thinking of sheep having sex."

"Well , perhaps you should think of us having sex, alla pecorina, instead? Far more interesting." He winked at her and she glared at him before she slipped inside her room, slamming the door tight behind her and locking it to ensure no surprise attacks from him in the middle of the night. She was done dealing with Lorenzo Romeo's friendly— more like hostile—overtures.

Chapter Thirteen

THE crew arrived and spent much of the day getting acquainted with the palazzo and meeting with anyone who could assist them. They set up a workspace in a guest house on the property, where they could have privacy to review the raw footage at the end of each day and make sure the edits would properly sync together.

Late in the afternoon, Justin sat at a custom-tiled table on the terrace, jotting down notes and enjoying *aperitivo* with a glass of reserve Chianti, when Sophie walked in.

"So far, so good, boss. Made even better by this amazing wine." He held up the glass of wine Fabiana had offered him.

"I think this is going to be fabulous," she said, crossing her arms and nibbling on her thumbnail.

"What do you think about Mr. Surly?" he said. "Hot but untouchable, literally and figuratively."

Sophie rolled her eyes and tapped her front tooth with her fingernail. "Like it or not, that one—I think he's going to be perfect. Our audience will eat him up like sweet cream on a silver spoon. Even if I'd rather spit him out like a sip of turned wine."

She didn't dare mention that an itty, bitty part of her would likely be front and center in line, ready to lap him right up. After all, she'd seen that thing of his in the light of day, and she'd bet money he could work wonders with it. In a way, it was sort of sad that she'd miss out on it. But that would just have to be, for all eternity. No way would she ever do that to herself.

"I'll take your word for it, but the way he goes around with that eviscerating scowl on his face, he's kind of a little bitch boy."

Sophie laughed. "I'm sure he'd love to hear that impression of him."

"Well, I know, but we're aiming to find some usable man parts while we're here. After all, it's Italy. Land of *amore* and all that stuff. I don't even care about the love part—I'm totally down with just lust."

"And you don't lust after him, even if he is being somewhat unpleasant?"

"Two strikes against him: he's not gay and he's a prick. Next!"

Sophie laughed. "Maybe we can get Tomasso to tap into the local talent and find someone for you."

"And while he's at it for you, too."

Sophie waved her arm. "I'm not kidding—I don't have time for that anyhow. I've got a career to advance. Besides, to hell with annoying men."

"I'll be sure to remind you of that next time you're moaning that you need a guy," Justin said. "Ah, but look who's here! The lovebirds."

He moved in between Gisele and Tomasso, draping an arm over each of their shoulders. "So what say we put our heads together and find someone who could provide a little companionship for your friends Justin and Sophie. All work and no play make us dull producers."

"Or something like that," Sophie said. "Thanks, but I don't need any matchmaking assistance."

"You're in Italia. Of course you need some amore," Tomasso said.

"I'm here for work, folks. Besides, not a good idea to mix business with pleasure. If I'm desperate, I can always find my friend Bob."

Justin waved his hand at her. "Are you kidding me? You're going to tell me you'd be satisfied with a battery-operated toy over the real McCoy?"

"Hey, that rhymes!" Gisele reached for Tomasso's hand. "And yes, sometimes a girl goes through dry spells and has to resort to a little double-A battery-assisted romance." She and Sophie fist-bumped.

"*Mi dispiace.* So sorry, but no way does that compare to the real thing." Tomasso furrowed his brow.

"What real thing?" Lorenzo said as he walked into the room, taking a swig from a bottle of water.

Sophie blanched and glanced away as if by looking in a different direction, he wouldn't see her.

"The women were trying to convince me and Justin that they're as happy with a vibrator as with a man."

Lorenzo choked on his water.

"Whoa, *mio fratello.*" Tomasso gave his back a few firm whacks in an attempt to stop the choking. "Be careful."

Lorenzo held up his hands as if in surrender. "I'm all right, Tomasso. I guess that took me off-guard, the notion that any woman would prefer some extremely loud, buzzing, plastic thing to a warm, hard, pulsating man." He fixed his gaze on Sophie.

She gave him a cold stare. "Yeah well, when that thing in your pants can come close to purring like a jet engine, give me a ring. Until then…" She flared her nostrils as she spoke.

Gisele stuck her finger in the air and made a hissing sound as if sizzling on a stove. "For the win, Soph."

The women laughed.

Justin held his hands up in a T, like a referee indicating a time-out. "Sorry, ladies. I have to go with the men here. Ain't nothing like a hot man on a cold night."

He, Sophie, and Gisele cracked up.

"Which reminds me, I know you fellas don't bat for the home team, but I was thinking you possibly know a guy nearby who might. I'd be much obliged if you could find someone."

Tomasso looked at Lorenzo. "You thinking who I'm thinking of?"

Lorenzo nodded. "Gareth. I could totally see it."

"Gareth?" Justin said, arching his brow. "Sounds very British, like he would be a palace insider or something. They're always the gay ones."

"Close," Tomasso said. "He was a palace insider with our cousins in Monaforte. Though now he's running a decorating business in Monaforte. Not that I look at these things, but I gotta tell you, he's pretty hot."

"Do tell. I need more info: hairs, eyes, build. Give me something to dream about."

"Hmmm, I don't know what you'd call the hair color." Tomasso paused, thinking. "A cross between blond and brown. Maybe sort of butterscotch. Which might make you think I'm a decorator, referring to a hair color as butterscotch. Disregard that. I think he has brown eyes. And he works out a ton so, yeah, I'm sure you'll not mind him. As far as men go, he's pretty easy on the eyes."

"As easy as this one here?" Justin pointed to Lorenzo, who cringed.

"Please, Justin, no more talking up the talent. He gets squeamish with any references to his looks. Or maybe it bloats his already generous ego." Sophie gave Justin an exaggerated wink.

"Apologies. Don't want to typecast you. So if you two could maybe figure out a way for me to meet him?"

"How would you feel about a blind date?"

"Honey, it beats another night on Grinder. I'd be on that like white on rice."

"I'll reach out to my cousins and see if we can get him down here on the train," Tomasso said. "We can all go to dinner in Florence. Sound good?"

"Sounds divine," Justin said. "Now let's try to help ugly up your brother so he isn't too paranoid—or is it vain—about his looks." He poked at Lorenzo's hair and tried to rub a little dirt on his face.

"Dinner in Florence it is. With a little luck, Justin can go with Gareth, Gisele's my date, and Sophie, you can bring your vibrator. I'm sure it will love the tiramisu where we're going."

They all laughed at her and she took it in stride.

"Seriously, all kidding aside, I propose that my ugly brother, Lorenzo, the most beastly of the Romeo brothers, be a gentleman and kindly escort Sophie for our group dinner. Lorenzo?"

Lorenzo caught Tomasso's eyes and glared hard, the muscles in his jaw visibly ticking. "Fine. But it can't be a late night. I've got things to do the next morning."

"Brava! Let's call up our forest friends and line up the pumpkin carriage and footmen mice. Our little Cinderella is going on a date with her very own Prince Charming."

Sophie buried her face in her hands, worried about what she'd been railroaded into. "Please, Justin. Get it straight. I'll need my best asbestos dress to keep from being burned because you're all forcing me out for the night with the Prince of Darkness. I hear it gets awfully warm the closer you get to hell."

Chapter Fourteen

TOMASSO volunteered to drive everyone in his SUV, which meant Gisele sat up front and Sophie drew the short straw and had to sit wedged between Lorenzo and Justin since they were meeting Gareth at the restaurant.

"This brings to mind family road trips with me stuffed in the middle between my two brothers when I was a kid," she grumbled.

"You think this is bad, try doing that with seven kids like we did when we were young," Tomasso said. "Moving our family around—which didn't happen often, mind you—was like a logistical nightmare. At least we don't have too far to go."

Although the distance they did have to drive included windy mountain roads, and with each switchback, Sophie found herself fighting gravity to avoid ending up tipping sideways into Lorenzo's lap. He was busy on his phone flirting on Facebook, or maybe opening up his Tinder app in anticipation of its usage upon arrival in Florence, and wouldn't even engage in conversation with her, which was fine. Except Tomasso swerved to avoid smacking into a wild boar scrambling across the road and Sophie found herself reaching for purchase, which ended up being on Lorenzo's crotch. At least *that* made him look up from his phone, even though Sophie pulled her hand away as quickly as she would have had she put it to the flame of a cooktop.

"Please, cara," he said with one of those smirks that made her want to box his ear. She couldn't believe his irksomeness made her think of the archaic phrase as though she were a schoolmarm in *Little House on the Prairie*. Box his ear. Oy. She was losing her New York edge and it had only been a few days. "No need to move away so suddenly. You can keep your hand there if you want."

Her lip snarled in disgust and she tugged her violet pashmina wrap a little tighter to her chest, feeling the need to close herself off physically from the man.

"So, Justin, you ready to meet your mystery date?" She tried to change the subject.

"Girl, I'm just happy to get out of the house for a while. It's a gorgeous place but sometimes you need to get away."

She rolled her eyes. "Tell me about it." Only problem was her getting away included still being with the thing she needed to get away from.

For the past few days, the crew had been shooting establishing shots around the palazzo, Romeo headquarters, and throughout the vineyard. They'd also brought in a drone to do some overhead shots, which so far looked spectacular. Meanwhile Sophie had spent much of the past couple of days rewriting the script and meeting individually with each of the Romeos who would appear in the program. The only one she'd avoided meeting with was Lorenzo. Of course he was going to be the main interview subject. Even though it had been established while planning the show, she was almost afraid to remind him he'd be the face of the Romeos.

She decided she'd line up as much as she could before even attempting to deal with him. She could only imagine what it would be like to get him to prep with the hair and makeup people. He would freak out the minute someone tried to put some bronzer or eyebrow gel on him. Though the makeup artists were both attractive women, and more than likely he'd be hitting them up for a fling by the time they dragged a brush through his hair or dabbed foundation on his skin. Not that she cared; he could hook up with whoever he wanted to. She simply needed to get this show filmed and wrapped so that her career wasn't balancing on the precipice. She had to prove to Danny that she could carry her own show and do it spectacularly well.

Maybe after all this was over she and Lorenzo could laugh about it. But probably not. He'd more than likely run her over with that miserable motorcycle of his.

"Gareth is the shit," Tomasso said as he drove them across a bridge entering the city. "I think you two are going to hit it off, *amico mio*. I must admit I'm pretty good at picking a good pairing if I do say so." He grinned at Gisele.

Lorenzo glared at him. "Don't even get any ideas, Tomasso."

Tomasso smiled and put a pointer finger in his cheek, feigning innocence. "Why Lorenzo, whatever ideas would I get? After all, I'm well aware of your bachelor status. Far be it from me to be up in your business."

"You know precisely what I'm talking about," Lorenzo said as he instructed his brother to avoid some road construction by turning a few blocks sooner than intended. It helped to be a Romeo in Florence as they were able to get waivers to drive and park pretty much wherever they wanted in the city, despite many restrictions for both. He found a space less than a block from the restaurant, *Il Lupo Affamato*, The Hungry Wolf.

Exiting the SUV was going to be a challenge for Sophie—she didn't want to have that awkward moment with her dress flying up and her barely there thong exposed for the locals—not to mention Lorenzo—to see as she tried to dismount from the oversized vehicle. She shifted to slide out on Justin's side because Justin had seen it before and she didn't care if he did, but the door had already been closed behind her. The safety lock meant she couldn't open it.

She frowned and shifted toward the door from which Lorenzo exited, only to see the grump standing there drumming his fingers on the door frame, looking as if he was waiting for the doctor to hurry up and finish the colonoscopy. What a jerk. Well, fine. If he was bored, she'd give him a show. She pulled off her pashmina, wrapped it around her purse, and thrust it into Lorenzo's hands so she'd be free to grab the handle above the door frame. Carefully she attempted to shift her way out of the car. Why was it much easier sliding in than exiting?

Lorenzo stood in front of the door frame, his eyes growing wider as she managed to make her way to the edge of the car, her arm clasping the handle above her, the other outstretched behind her. She worried her boobs might spill right out of the sexy little dress she'd worn and laughed to herself. It would serve Lorenzo right. *Look don't touch, sucker.*

She managed to climb out of the vehicle with a hint of dignity left and grabbed her shawl and purse from Lorenzo as she straightened her dress, adjusted her breasts, and joined the others on the sidewalk.

Holy shit. Lorenzo could barely keep his tongue from lolling out of his mouth upon seeing what Sophie had been hiding beneath that shawl of hers. She wore a gray dress made up of some sort of stretchy fabric that plunged deep to her cleavage in such a way that the bottom left a good four-inch gap between each breast. The stretchy gray fabric acted almost like a hammock for each tit. *Mamma mia.*

She had a strand of pearls draped twice; the longer strand dipped well into that gap between her breasts, its ready access to them almost taunting him. Meanwhile, her hair up in a messy bun made her neck go on forever, like the road to the Promised Land, only he wasn't allowed to enter it. More like the Road to Perdition, but damn, it would almost be worth being doomed there forever. Almost.

Her slender waist was emphasized by a wide band of stretchy white fabric, and the bottom of the dress flared out into a skirt that ended above the knee, showing off those long, lean legs of hers. Jesus, those legs. When she was sliding out of the car, he wanted so badly to graze his palms along the smooth surface of her shapely calves, gradually inching his hands upward. Destination: whatever lay beneath that flimsy skirt.

For a minute, Lorenzo was frozen, trying to imagine what he wanted to do first with her. Maybe go for the breasts—they would be an easy get considering the design of the thing she was wearing. All he'd need to do is slip his fingers along the fabric edge and he'd be in, cupping those magnificent breasts in each of his greedy palms. He'd way rather have that in his hands than his dick, which at the rate things were going, would be his fate upon their return to the palazzo tonight. Again. If he could last that long.

Part of him wanted to grab those pearls and give a tug, seeking vengeance for that damned jewelry being able to linger precisely where he wanted to. Maybe he could help her retrieve the pearls as they spilled into that fabric that was barely concealing her tits.

But the bigger part of him wanted to lift up that skirt and see what—if anything—was lurking beneath her outfit. She must have known it was killing him by inches. Although speaking of inches, dammit, for what seemed like the millionth time since her arrival, he was growing by inches, like it or not.

God, the woman had him by the balls and didn't even know it. Or maybe she did. He took a deep breath and tried to concentrate on anything other than *quelle tette perfette*. Those perfect tits. He knew agreeing to this dinner had been a bad mistake. He was going to have to concentrate on something else throughout the meal. Maybe ruminating on a possible budding romance between Justin and Gareth would pour enough cold water on his libido to get him through the night. Not that he had anything against two dudes falling for each other. He was perfectly comfortable with his own sexuality and not at all threatened by men having differing preferences. But it wasn't something that got him hot and bothered like Sophie clearly did. Surely it could be an antidote to her presence.

If it wasn't, then he was in trouble. Because right now,

all he wanted to do was take her right there in front of the whole restaurant, smack-dab on top of the table. It felt like the only way to ultimately purge thoughts of her from his mind. Crap, he was in deep trouble.

Chapter Fifteen

SOPHIE grabbed a seat as far away from Lorenzo as possible while remaining at the same six-top table. That was all fine and good until Tomasso insisted on seat assignments.

Gisele leaned in to whisper in her ear. "It's so that Gareth and Justin can be closer to each other. You understand, right?"

Sophie heaved a sigh. Far be it from her to throw a wrench in the future Mr. and Mr. Justin Magruder. Or whatever that Gareth guy's name was.

"Can you at least sit between me and the cranky one?"

"If we do that it messes up the whole seating flow," she said. "Plus I want to be next to Tomasso. And I want to be right by Justin so I can eavesdrop on what's going on."

Sophie rolled her eyes. "Great. Leave me next to the guy who won't talk to me all night. Perfect. Wake me when it's done. I'll be the one with crumbs all over my lap from gorging on breadsticks since I had nothing else to do."

Gisele poked her. "Silly. He'll be fine. I'll get Tomasso to say something to him."

"Ugh, I think that'll make things worse. He's like a skunk—the more you bother him the more you'll live to regret it."

"He doesn't smell like a skunk, I can tell you that."

Sophie had to give her that much. He smelled like a combination of hot, sexy man and hot, sexy man who was busted wanking off. Because she recognized whatever cologne he had on tonight was the same one that wafted from him that first afternoon... He was all dressed and ready for dinner when she'd first encountered him—more like when he encountered her. Maybe he was ready to go out afterward even, so he made sure he smelled great yet somehow took a detour back to his room afterward to take care of vital business...

Whatever it was, the woodsy, musky, citrusy smell of him instantly evoked images of a very naked Lorenzo and made her a little wistful that he wasn't fair game. Because if he was, she would not only have sat next to him gladly but might have settled in his lap after a few drinks to get socially lubricated. Or more like physically lubricated.

Tomasso and Lorenzo spoke to the restaurant owner in Italian—that was another thing. Every word out of Lorenzo's mouth was like verbal sex. It was arousing to listen to. She could listen to him talk all day long and mentally swoon as he did it. Of course it was much better when he spoke Italian because when he spoke to her in English, it was frequently less than pleasant. Whatever.

Gareth arrived and introductions were made all around. Sophie winked at Justin who looked happy as a bunny eating lettuce. Good. The man passed the looks test. Would be great if Justin would find a fun little Italian diversion for the next few weeks. Then they'd all be happy. Well, Justin and Gisele would be. And Sophie already was happy, what with her own show and all. Her life couldn't be more perfect.

The waiter arrived with a bottle of prosecco, quickly pouring a glass for each of them. Tomasso raised his flute. "To friends, old and new. And to Sophie, here's hoping your show is a raging success."

Sophie blushed—she hated being the center of attention and sure, they were all gathered here because of this show. Still, it didn't feel like it was all about her. She was a mere cog in the wheel. But she looked over and saw Lorenzo roll his eyes and suddenly she was more than happy to be the showstopper for the evening if it meant taking another dig at him.

"Thanks, Tomasso. And everyone, for all your help. And especially you, Lorenzo. I mean I don't know what this little hayseed from America would do without your amazing guidance." She batted her eyelashes in a mocking manner and Gisele and Justin laughed. One thing Sophie was not was a hayseed from the middle of nowhere. Born and raised in New York, a product of Long Island, the woman would plow you down like a ride-on mower if you crossed her the wrong way. In some ways it was surprising she'd not done that with Lorenzo yet. *Give me time*, she thought. *Give me time.* For now, she decided the most fun she could have was to tease the crap out of him. She could tell it would make him nuts if she were to taunt him with her wares. He was a man, after all.

"Can I interest you in some?" Sophie said, thrusting her breasts toward Lorenzo, leaning slightly forward, revealing as much cleavage as possible as she passed a platter of antipasti.

Lorenzo gulped. His brother had ordered the meal to be served family style, but any more of this and it would quickly become X-rated, certainly not suitable for families and small children. He couldn't help but ogle them, resting as they were so close to the platter. If he were a restaurateur, he'd have her serve those breasts atop a platter and be done with it. Because all he now had an appetite for was to suck on those things.

He closed his eyes and counted to ten. Invoked a mental image of Cupid spearing Gareth and Justin with an arrow. If that was how it worked—did they both have to get impaled on the same arrow for true love to occur? He had no experience when it came "true love" with the exception of his parents. Of course he'd seen the danger of what happened when you loved too hard. It was impossible when that love was lost. He knew that was never going to be for him.

"Grazie mille. I'd like nothing more." He served himself slices of lardo di colonnata, some prosciutto, insalata di carciofi e grana—he could not get enough of local artichokes in season with parmiggiano cheese—a little bit of soprassata, and some crostini toscani. At least if he was busy eating he could avoid making small talk with her.

The din of conversation from the other end of the table had escaped him until now.

"And Sophie, damn, that dress, it's something else. Isn't it? What do you think, Lorenzo?" Tomasso cocked his brow.

Lorenzo was going to kill his brother the minute he had a chance. The dude was having far too much fun yanking him around. And he knew why: he was seeking revenge for his own lost bet. Lorenzo knew he had to stay strong. He could do it. There was nothing special about Sophie. Well, nothing he couldn't find on twenty other women. If he looked hard.

"Lorenzo?" Tomasso pressed his brother.

Lorenzo set his knife and fork down. "Sophie looks amazing, Tomasso. Is that what you were looking for me to say? That she looks downright fuckable?"

Justin choked on a sip of wine. Gareth glanced at him. "What the hell's that all about?"

Justin shrugged.

Gisele tried to dispel the tension in the air. "Oh, Lorenzo, Tomasso told me you love to play games with everyone. Like you love to say something super outlandish that no one would expect you to say, simply to see how everyone reacts. For a second there that surprised me. But now I realize you were just messing with everyone. Good one!" She knit her brow as she glanced over at Sophie, who was busy munching on a piece of fava bean bruschetta, apparently not even paying attention to the conversation.

Mercifully the waiter arrived with the primi piatti: plates of spaghetti al pomodoro, a ravioli al sugo di coniglio, and a tagliatelle ai funghi. As Sophie passed the rabbit ravioli she leaned toward Lorenzo and whispered so only he could hear, "So you find me fuckable?"

It was Lorenzo's turn to choke. "Mi dispiace molto, cara. That was my brother trying to get a rise out of me. I'm afraid he succeeded."

She looked down at his lap and frowned. "And here I

thought I was the one who had gotten a rise out of you." She turned away to talk to Gareth, seated to her right.

"I hear Monaforte is a lovely country," she said, not missing a beat.

"It's lovely. You should come visit before you return to the States."

"I'd love to," she said. "I'm sure Gisele won't leave Tomasso's side, but maybe I can talk Justin into taking the train up with me. Oh, except then I'll be the third wheel, yet again."

"Oh, honey, trust me, there are so many gorgeous men in Monaforte. Maybe I can even find you a prince or a marchese for a day or two."

"She hardly needs to go to Monaforte to find a marchese," Lorenzo said. "That's the title each of us has been given."

"Yes but I'm looking for someone interesting and fun." Sophie turned back to Gareth. "Let's do that. And I'm flexible: it can be a duke or an earl, or even a lowly lord." She winked.

"Oh, so you're an equal opportunity gold digger?" Lorenzo said.

"You know what they say. When in Toscano…" She placed her fist up to her mouth and discreetly flipped Lorenzo the finger.

Gareth laughed and gave her a thumbs-up.

"All I know is I'm glad I didn't get seated between the two of you," he said. "I'm afraid I'd have combusted by now. And the night is still young for me—I don't want to incinerate as collateral damage over whatever crazy stuff is happening with the two of you before I get to know Justin a little better."

"Trust me, there is absolutely nothing between the two of us but mutual disdain. You are one hundred percent safe from any sort of combusting. I, on the other hand, truly should have donned that heat-protective clothing, what with me being forced to the seventh circle of hell and all."

She reached for a bottle of Romeo Chianti and refilled her glass. The only way she was going to get through this was with ample reinforcements of the fortified grape variety.

Chapter Sixteen

LUCKY for the rest of the table, the *secondi* arrived, and conversation turned to food. For the duration of the meal, Lorenzo refrained from any interaction that would cause more friction. He ate his meal and mostly kept his mouth shut.

"This steak is un-freaking-believable," Justin said as he cut a bite-sized portion of his meat.

"It's *bistecca alla fiorentina*," Tomasso said. It's a speciality in *Firenze*. *Molto buono*, no?"

"Wait'll you try the *dolce*." Gareth pointed to the dessert menu that was written on a chalkboard on the wall. "The choices are endless but if it was up to me, it's a toss-up between the *affogato*, which is basically ice cream drowned with a shot of hot espresso, or the tiramisu. And how can you ever go wrong with tiramisu?"

Sophie patted her stomach. "Sorry, no room at the inn. I don't think I've eaten this much in one sitting since, well, since my parents announced they were getting a divorce when I was fourteen."

"That bad, was it?" Gareth said. "Mine split up when I was a baby. At least I missed the drama."

"You don't even know the half of it," Sophie said. "It's a toss-up if it was harder to live with them together or dealing with the tension of the two of them apart. Oh, or when they got back together again. Or when they split up again. You get my drift."

"I think it was Mae West who said 'marriage is an institution. I'm just not ready for the institution yet.' A wise woman, she was. No institution for me, either," Lorenzo said with a sly wink.

Tomasso and Gareth started to laugh. "Our little renegade. Roaming eyes, roaming heart," Tomasso said.

"I'm just wise, is all."

"Well, I'm going to be wise and ask for a doggy bag for what's left on my plate before I burst," Sophie said.

Lorenzo scowled.

"What?" She wrinkled her brow at him.

"You're in Italy, cara. We don't do 'doggy bags' here." He made air quotes for emphasis. They didn't do doggy bags, but they sure did doggy style. That's what kept drifting through his brain as he tried to focus on anything other than sex with that damned woman.

"Well big damned deal. I'm sure they can scrounge up a piece of aluminum foil in the kitchen to wrap this to go. I'm too full to eat, I'd like to take it for later."

Tomasso held up his hand to his brother to stop him from continuing the discussion and motioned for the waiter. "*La signora* would like to bring this home, please."

Lorenzo rolled his eyes and wondered whatever happened to the concept of *when in Rome.*

Sophie was feeling no pain by the time they walked back to the car. Well, her strappy Manolo Blahnik sandals might have been causing a little bit of pain. But they were worth it because they looked super sexy with her dress. She only hoped Lorenzo Romeo was eating his heart out having to look, not touch.

"Almost forgot we have an extra passenger for the ride back, which means we need to do some creative seat arranging," Tomasso said. He looked at their party, and pointing his finger, did a head count to be sure. "So that means, hmmm. Let's see. Justin, you're a little bit smaller, so you sit in the middle. Gareth you can sit in the passenger seat behind Gisele. Lorenzo, I'm putting you behind the driver's seat, which leaves Sophie—would you mind terribly if you sat on Lorenzo's lap? It's not that long of a drive back."

It was hard to tell whose face fell faster: Sophie's or Lorenzo's. Needless to say, Sophie was not thrilled with the suggestion. Was Tomasso trying to make her life a living hell? On the one hand, it might be fun to torment Lorenzo the whole way back. Then again, he was so disagreeable, he'd probably make cracks about her being too heavy. She knew she wasn't, but still. Couldn't she just sit on Justin's lap? Although then she'd have to sit splayed atop him in the middle seat, which wouldn't work. Plus she did want to help Justin have some time with Gareth in the back seat, and if she was parked on top of him, she'd effectively kill that. Besides, she didn't want to be a nuisance to Tomasso, especially since he'd picked up the slack where Lorenzo continued to fall short.

"Could you maybe strap me to the roof rack?" Sophie tried to make light of the situation since she figured she was stuck regardless.

"Nah, too many bugs would stick to you and ruin that pretty dress." Tomasso grinned.

She plastered a tepid smile across her face. The kind of smile you wear when your mother is going to force you to go the school dance with the boy who hasn't washed his hair in a week but who asked you months before anyone else would even think to.

"Let's hear it for Soph, taking one for the team." Gisele lifted her hands like a cheerleader holding pom-poms.

Sophie shook her head, realizing she'd lost the fight if there ever was one.

It took a few minutes to get everyone adequately seated, like arranging pieces to a puzzle when one piece belongs to an entirely different puzzle. Finally Sophie found herself having to decide whether she would straddle Lorenzo with her back to him, but that felt a little too much like a Kama Sutra pose.

Her only other choice was to ride sort of sidesaddle, which did mean that her boobs were going to be at eye level with Lorenzo's face. That was no skin off her back and might make him slightly crazy. At least the ride would be more interesting...

"Um, what about a seat belt, people?" Sophie said. For the most part, she was a rule-follower; she was never one of those teens who piled into cars with fourteen kids and no seat belts on. She also didn't start campfires if Smoky the Bear told her not to.

"*Calmarsi*, signora," Lorenzo said.

"What's he saying to me?"

"Calm down, lady," Gareth piped in.

"Well, that's fine for him to say but I'm the one who will be the projectile going through the windshield if one of those wild boars runs in front of us again—not him.

"*Calma*," he said. Relax.

As if it was going to be possible to relax while she sat in his lap and smelled the fragrant aroma of hot—yet vexing—man beneath her.

Chapter Seventeen

LORENZO was decidedly not going to get all hot and bothered by the two guys next to him shoving their tongues down each other's throats like a couple of teenagers late at night on a park bench. It seemed to happen the instant they were away from the city lights and on the mountainous road home. It sure didn't take those two long to become better acquainted.

On second thought, maybe Tomasso should have made *them* share a seat. As it was they were steaming up the windows. Between them and the quiet moans coming from the front seat—where he guessed Tomasso was doing a little passenger-seat entertainment with his girlfriend—it felt more like a swap party than a friendly ride home.

That left him with the princess perched on her throne, and that throne happened to be him. Impossibly turned on by the woman whose breasts heaved perilously close to his mouth about every five to seven seconds, he felt cursed. She'd been his curse ever since she came on the scene, and once again he found himself hard and wanting, this time painfully so. He wondered if she could tell beneath that flimsy, barely there dress how much his body responded to her being there. Even though it would respond to pretty much anyone sitting on his lap. Well, anyone who looked like her, at any rate.

They could not have arrived back at the palazzo soon enough. After Tomasso eventually helped ease Sophie out of the car, Lorenzo stayed behind to settle things down—either that or he'd be the victim of much abuse from his brother and Gareth, which was the last thing he needed.

Sophie felt like a gigantic third wheel with the paired-off couples heading toward their little happy place. She was eternally grateful that Lorenzo stayed back instead of returning to the house when she did.

She bade goodnight to Tomasso and Gisele, then to Gareth and Justin—Lord knew if they were headed to separate quarters but it wasn't her place to ask—and diverted to the kitchen to put her doggy bag in the large commercial refrigerator. She hoped it wasn't weird to be sticking her dinky little foil packet of leftover veal in there. For all she knew, it would end up in the dog's bowl for breakfast.

When she opened the large door, staring her in the face was a large tray of tiramisu, which looked ten times more delicious than the one at the restaurant, even though that one had been quite a challenge to resist. And though she'd felt full an hour ago, her stomach was suddenly growling and it seemed the best idea to maybe have a teensy taste of the dessert. Since it had already been served to people, she figured she could take a fat scoop out with her fingers and no one would be the wiser.

She dragged her pointer and middle fingers along the part where it had been cut into and brought the creamy treat to her mouth, first licking her fingers, then sucking both fingers into her mouth to savor the remaining bits. She let out a moan.

"Oh, my God. This is way better than sex," she said, unable resist digging in for another taste.

That moan. Alarms went off in Lorenzo's head the minute he heard it coming from the kitchen. He could never hear that sound again without picturing it coming from Sophie's soft lips when he found her in such a state of extended pleasure. He had no choice but to follow where it led him.

He opened the door to the kitchen and there she was, her fingers plunged deep into a pan of his mamma's tiramisu, moaning about how superior it was to sex. As if. Clearly the woman knew not of what she spoke because even the worst sex he'd ever had was at least a thousand times better than a simple dessert.

"Poor, deprived woman," Lorenzo said, causing Sophie to freeze with her fingers in her mouth, eyes wide as dinner plates. "To think anyone could fancy a platter of dessert to be even remotely comparable to having sex." He shook his head.

Sophie turned, the tray in her hand, and stuck her

fingers in again. "You know what, Lorenzo? I've had a few glasses of wine and I'm feeling fine. So I'm not going to let you get under my skin. In fact, I feel a need to prove you wrong. Here, taste for yourself." She hollowed out another chunk of the dessert and extended her arm toward him. She nodded. "Go ahead. I'm not going to bite you. Have a taste."

She held her fingers in front of his mouth as he eyed her, like a cat trying to decide whether to pounce on a nearby squirrel or keep on walking.

At last, he swiped his tongue along her finger, and she cocked her brow waiting for his reaction. Within seconds his mouth closed around her two fingers and he sucked hard as he coaxed his tongue along them.

"I've had my mamma's tiramisu a thousand times, but never has it tasted quite this good." His mouth tilted to a grin on one side as he helped himself to a scoop of the dessert, offering it up to Sophie. Her gaze traveled from his offering to his eyes and back again before she finally swiped her tongue along his fingers. It didn't take Lorenzo long to join her, their tongues meeting along his ring finger before their mouths pressed together. No longer concerned about licking his fingers clean, he pulled Sophie toward him as their tongues clashed in a heated frenzy. Sophie scooped more and inserted it between their lips and Lorenzo sucked and licked and moaned.

Finally he pulled away from her, but only for better access. "Fuck, cara," he said, tugging her shawl off and tossing it onto the floor. Next came those two breast-filled hammocks that had taunted him the whole night through. He pulled one off her shoulder, then the other, exposing her breasts for him to feast on. His mouth immediately fastened onto one already-hard nipple, where he sucked and nipped until Sophie called out his name.

He grabbed the tiramisu, placed it on the marble countertop, and dug in with his fingers, smearing the sticky treat across her breast. With lust-crazed eyes, he stared into Sophie's eyes for a second before pressing her up against the door of the refrigerator and burrowing back down to lick her breasts clean.

"*Bellissima,*" Lorenzo said as he planted his mouth over hers, pressing himself against her, his hands racing over her body, up beneath her dress, sliding beneath her thong. "*La tua figa è così umida,*" he hummed in her ear. "Your pussy is so wet."

Sophie wrapped a leg around his waist, drawing him closer as she lifted his shirt out from his pants.

Suddenly he pulled away. "Mio Dio, carissima," he said, extending his hand and linking it with hers. "*Andiamo. Prontissimo.*"

Sophie wasn't quite sure what all he was saying to her but it sounded fantastic coming out of his mouth, and whatever it was, the urgency with which he spoke was the same language that her own body was talking, prontissimo indeed.

Chapter Eighteen

LORENZO could not recall a time he felt so desperate to get inside a woman's hot, wet body as he did right now with Sophie the producer whose last name he couldn't for the life of him even recall. Not that it mattered. Who cared about surnames at a time like this? He raced down the empty corridor, panting, whether from the pace of their running or the urgency of their needs. They arrived at the entrance to their respective rooms and he pulled her toward hers.

"Since the minute I saw you in here, I've wanted to take you, right there, just as I saw you, your face flushed, your pink nipples hard, your hips gyrating." He opened the door and they raced in, slamming the door behind them.

He shrugged off his jacket and wasted no time undressing Sophie, reaching behind to slide the zipper down, shifting the dress from her hips, where it fell to the floor in a hush. Her hands trembled as she loosened his tie and undid each of the buttons on his shirt, eventually tossing it by the door.

Lorenzo stood back and stared at this witch of a woman standing before him in nothing but a tiny stretch of black fabric that covered her beautifully smooth pussy and those hot, hot sandals that emphasized her amazing, long legs.

He motioned with his finger for her to turn around. He didn't want to miss anything about her: the lines of her beautiful back, the soft curve of her sexy ass. She was fucking beautiful, and suddenly he couldn't for the life of him understand why he had been combative with her. Make love, not war. That should be his motto. Why fight with someone as stunning as Sophie Pellegrino—*aha! that was her name!*—when he could be driving his cock into her instead?

Sophie reached for his belt, quickly unfastening it, then unbuttoned his pants and pulled down his zipper, tugging his pants over his ass.

It was her turn to stand back and take him in, eyes widening at the sight of him. Lorenzo stood there, his cock straining desperately against his black bikini briefs. She twirled her finger, mimicking his demand from moments earlier, and he smiled at her cheekiness, turning obligingly.

But his patience was wavering; he needed to touch her, lick her, suck her, so he pressed against her, his knee pushing between her legs as their lips met. He whispered sweet nothings into her ear in Italian. "I want to fuck your sweet pussy," he said, which always sounds much better as "*voglio scopare la tua figa dolce.*"

He dragged his tongue across her lips, along her chin, up to her ear, nipping on her ear lobe, then the shell of her ear, his tongue following along it until his mouth was over her ear, and he moaned and breathed hard as he tweaked her nipples with his fingers. His tongue resumed its lazy meandering downward, along the column of her neck, pausing at the nape, where he licked in circles. Dragging his tongue farther down her cleavage and circling first one breast, then the other, he flicked her nipple and settled his lips over the top of it sucking hard. Sophie groaned, and he soon repeated it on the other one.

His tongue continued its downward momentum, pausing to circle her navel while his fingers tugged off her thong. He sat back on his knees and admired her naked body. "Spread your legs, cara."

She did as he told her, allowing him to resume his efforts, taking his time, dragging his tongue along her creases, circling her clit, and burying it deep inside her, mimicking what he planned to do with his cock as soon as he brought her to climax.

Sophie swirled her fingers through Lorenzo's thick hair, pressing him toward her, encouraging him with her hands and her sounds of pleasure. Lorenzo stroked long, slow passes along her labia while his fingers slid inside, curling forward in search of her G-spot. Next he fastened his lips over her clit and sucked hard. He could sense the flutter of her internal muscles—they spasmed as she moaned loudly, her hips pressing into his mouth, her body shaking, legs trembling as Lorenzo steadied her. When she stopped trembling, he stood and wrapped his arms around her, pressing his hard length along her wet folds.

"Cara, allow me?" He cocked his eyebrow, desperate for her to say yes.

She nodded, pulling down his briefs. His cock stood proud and pulsing. "How do you want it, carissima?"

Sophie reached for his cock, wrapping her long fingers around it, stroking it rhythmically. She lifted an eyebrow. "Well," she said, "there's a vision I haven't been able to get out of my mind ever since you first mentioned it…"

He reached for his nearby pants, pulling his wallet

from a pocket, quickly finding a condom. Tossing the wallet down, he tore the condom out and handed it to Sophie to do the honors. As she unrolled it over his hard length, he groaned. "Cara, I'm not going to last long with your greedy hands on me like that. Tell me what you want."

She turned around, pressing her bottom up against his cock and rubbing. He reached his hands around to massage her tits, sighing at how good they felt in his hands. She glanced over her shoulder and smiled. "I was thinking maybe alla pecorina?"

"*Tesoro*," Lorenzo whispered. *Darling*. "You wish is my command."

Sophie climbed onto the bed and positioned herself on all fours and turned to smile at Lorenzo, who knelt down behind her, his hands worshipping her back and hips before settling on her ass. He slid his cock along her slick center and they both moaned at the touch of his hard warmth on her. He pressed his tip against her opening and slowly entered her, biting his lip against the pleasure as her pussy swallowed his length. Once he was buried deep inside her, he stilled, leaning forward to play with her tits. Slowly he withdrew and pressed in again, reaching down to feel where their bodies were joined.

"Cara, I can't believe how perfectly my cock fits your body. It's like it was made to be there."

Sophie moaned. "Lorenzo, fill me up, baby."

Which was all he needed to begin driving hard into her, pressing deep and grinding until his balls pressed up against her clit, his cock moving like a piston in and out, his fingers working her from the outside as his cock took care of filling her up just as she'd begged him to do.

"*Vengo*," he shouted. *I'm coming*. His body tensed and

he thrust deep and held himself still as he emptied himself into her right as he felt the contractions deep inside her, gripping his cock, milking it.

They collapsed with him still inside her, both breathing hard, their bodies coated in sweat and sticky residue from their little dessert foreplay.

"Now that, cara, was better than all the tiramisu in the world."

Chapter Nineteen

SOPHIE could not believe what a turn of fortune had occurred in such a short period of time. Only a few hours ago she was throwing Lorenzo dirty looks at dinner, and now she was naked with him in a shower as he gently washed gooey remnants of dessert off her breasts with his slick, soapy hands.

The Italian man's motto must have been "be prepared" because Lorenzo didn't even have to go back to his room to get a second condom, instead finding where he'd tossed his wallet on the floor and pulling one out for round two. Or at least she hoped it would be round two.

"As much as I love to lick those sweet tits, right now I'd much rather have the chance to soap you up and have my way with you with hot water running down our bodies."

What girl could turn down that proposition?

The shower had multiple showerheads, making it like a massive shower massage. Lorenzo took a spray nozzle and aimed it at her breasts, rinsing the sticky residue, then targeted her nipples. Sophie shuddered at the sensation.

He reached for the pins in her hair, pulling her tresses down to drape over her back. Wetting her hair before he poured shampoo into the palm of his hand, he slowly worked it through her scalp and downward, massaging it into a lather.

"Lean your head back so I can rinse, cara."

She was more than happy to lean in to this man—he had all the right moves and the most perfect touch.

After they'd toweled off they retreated to her bed.

"Now it's my turn," Sophie said as she ran her fingers along his hard torso. She planted kisses along his jaw and down his neck, dragging her tongue along his collarbone. She continued to lick her way to his chest, nipping on a nipple and trailing her mouth beneath his arm to that area that made her mad, swirling her tongue under his arm, trailing her fingertips through the hair there. Soon she migrated farther down his body, her tongue following the contours of his abs and the trail of hair that pointed the way to where she wanted to go.

She settled herself between his legs, cupped his cock in her hands, and fixed her gaze on his as she reached her tongue out and gave a long, slow swipe along the head. Her own personal sucker. Or was she his? He groaned and closed his eyes.

"*Grazie a dio.*" Thank God.

Sophie swirled her tongue over the swollen head of his dick, then worked it along the rim, taking several long licks from the base to the tip before closing her lips over the head and sliding it into her mouth. Lorenzo placed his hands on her head, guiding her, encouraging her with each long suck. He pressed himself toward her mouth, and again their eyes locked as she took him in deep while her hands pulled on him near the base of his penis.

"Cara, I can't last. I need to feel your wet warmth around me again." He pulled her up toward him and she straddled his body. He handed her the condom and together they rolled it onto his hard length; Sophie lowered herself onto his cock, his girth spreading her wide as he buried deep into her.

She stayed still for a moment, adjusting to his size, leaning forward so he could take her nipple into his mouth. Soon she ground her hips toward him, gyrating enough to rub her clit against his base. She began to lift and lower herself onto him, picking up the pace as he grabbed her ass and used the leverage to thrust into her. Sophie leaned forward and pressed her mouth to Lorenzo's, reveling in the sensation of being connected so deeply. She picked up the pace of her own gyrations. His cock kept hitting that perfect spot time and again, and within minutes she felt the burst of fireworks start from deep inside and spasms spreading out to squeeze Lorenzo's dick as she shouted out his name. He gripped her hard as he thrust himself into her again and again, finally letting out a loud groan and a shudder as he came inside her.

Sophie awoke to the sound of birdsong outside. It took her a moment to remember what had transpired… and it all came back in a rush of memories as she noticed tender places on her body that hadn't been sore in ages. The feeling made her as happy as those birds chirping to greet the morning. She extended her arm to feel for Lorenzo, but her hand came up empty. Instead all she found was a cold sheet.

Huh. Maybe he had to be somewhere early. Shame. She'd have loved to go for a little command performance. After all, he was right: tiramisu couldn't hold a candle to flat-out monkey sex, especially after a long dry spell.

Well, she had a busy day ahead of her. She only wished they'd discussed how they were going to handle this publicly. The fact was, she had no business sleeping with this man. But come off it—how could she not, under the circumstances? It would have taken the willpower of a superhero to resist the magnetic sexual pull he emitted.

Well, she'd simply take her cues from him and go from there.

"Buon giorno!" Sophie smiled as she joined those seated already for breakfast in the dining room.

"Ciao, Sophie." Valentina greeted her with a kiss on each cheek. "Have you met my brother Dominico yet?" Valentina pointed to a tall, solidly built man with the classic Romeo hair and stubble on his chin. The brothers all looked so similar, though without question, Lorenzo won the gene pool with perfect looks and a rockin' bod.

"So thrilled to meet you." She extended her hand to shake his, but he kissed her just as Valentina had.

"I've heard so much about you from my family," he said. "We're going to be celebrities on American television. Maybe this will help my art."

"Art?"

"Well, it's a little side thing that I do."

"Don't be humble, Dominico. What you do is really quite magical."

"I'm on pins and needles," Sophie said as she sat down across the table from him. "Do tell."

"I'm an artist, and my medium is flower petals."

Sophie thought for a minute. Once she saw a piece of artwork that was a giant butterfly, all composed of individual butterfly wings. Thinking about the poor butterflies that died for the cause had made her sort of sick to her stomach. Flower petals, though—she could get behind that.

"What exactly do you do with them?"

"In different parts of Italy, there are festivals in which Infiorate artists ply their craft. Using only the petals of flowers, we execute large-scale mural carpets along roadways and sidewalks, depicting all sorts of imagery. Often it has to do with religious things because many times the festivals linked to it are tied to Catholic holidays. It is Italy after all."

"I'd love to see your work. I guess it doesn't last long, does it?"

"That is the nature of the beast. It remains elusive. It will never hang in the Uffizi. But there are always photographs, videos on YouTube, that sort of thing."

"Better yet, you can see him at work at the Infiorate di Santa Romeo, which will be in a few days. Dominico's been hard at work preparing for this, which is why you didn't meet him until now."

"Grazie mille," Sophie said as a staffer gave her a cappuccino and cornetto. "This sounds exciting—I've never been to a festival in Italy and I hear they're amazing. All the religious leaders parading around with big staffs and carrying relics of saints, like preserved fingers and noses and such."

Valentina laughed. "When you put it that way it sounds a bit creepy."

Dominico arched his brow. "Valentina, they parade through villages carrying things like eight-hundred-year-old earlobes that someone at some point claimed belonged to a person who was burned at the stake or impaled by buffalo horns or Lord knows what other torture in the name of the Lord. You gotta admit, it is a bit macabre."

Valentina shrugged. "You got me there. Anyhow, Sophie, you have to come to the Infiorate di Santa Romeo. It's so much fun. There will be beautiful floral artwork, food galore, and of course wine. We don't do anything without wine. You can include something about it in the show!"

"I am definitely going to do that. It sounds so interesting and unique. I'm sure the audience will love it."

"What're they going to love?" Gisele strolled in arm in arm with Tomasso.

"This very cool thing we're going to in the village. Did you meet Dominico? Tomasso's brother makes these amazing murals with flower petals. We're going to make it part of the show."

"Sounds awesome. Hey—you hear anything yet from Justin this morning?"

"Luckily I'm not down the same corridor that he is—or you for that matter. I'm sure I'd not have slept a wink if I had been."

Sophie chose not to disclose that she'd hardly slept a

wink as it was.

"Now, now. Tomasso and I are discreet. I was just wondering—Justin and Gareth seemed to hit it off so instantly."

"Um, yeah. They certainly were fogging up the windows last night on the way home."

Gisele giggled. "I had hoped that was you and Lorenzo. We gave you every chance possible."

Sophie frowned. "You mean you did that on purpose?"

Gisele shrugged. "Well, not me exactly. Tomasso." She pointed a thumb at her boyfriend who was pouring an espresso from the nearby Nespresso machine.

"He was trying to get us together? Why?"

"Well, apart from it would be nice for you to have someone to do things with while you're here… Let's just say that Tomasso and Lorenzo have a history between them. They like to prove each other wrong, and often there is money on the table."

"So they made some bet that involved me?"

"Not you," Tomasso said. "Women in general. My brother prides himself on being certain he will never settle down. So much so he's willing to put a lot of money on the line to prove it. I figured I'd give him a little rope to perhaps hang himself with."

"Oh, great, then I'm basically part of some stupid game between brothers? Thanks but no thanks."

"It wasn't working anyhow—no need to get all upset about it." Gisele took a sip of her fresh-squeezed orange juice and licked her lips.

Sophie rolled her eyes. Wasn't working indeed.

"What wasn't working?" Lorenzo strolled into the

room. His hair was damp, and bits of it curled around the nape of his neck in that sexy way that makes a girl want to twirl her fingers in it. He had on a sage-green T-shirt and blue jeans. She wanted to find a quiet corner and touch him all over. But she didn't. Because now she knew she was just a joke between the brothers. She wanted nothing to do with that.

"Apparently Tomasso thought I would somehow sway your beliefs about relationships. Or something like that."

Tomasso was slicing his throat with his finger, indicating for Sophie to shut up.

Lorenzo squinted. "Oh he did, did he?"

She shrugged, not knowing what else to say.

"I've got one word for my brother, and maybe you could be so kind as to pass it on to him."

"Yeah, sure, I guess." Sophie had no idea how deep she was into this brotherly spat.

"*Fottiti.* Go ahead and pass that on to him."

"Fottiti?" she said out loud as Fabiana entered the room.

Chapter Twenty

"WHAT is going on in here? I walk in expecting a cheerful breakfast and people are hurling vulgarities at each other? You all should be ashamed of yourselves."

Sophie leaned over to Dominico. "Um, what exactly does fottiti mean?"

He grinned. "You sure you want to know?"

She nodded, frowning.

"Go fuck yourself."

Sophie cringed. She'd just shouted "go fuck yourself" in front of her genteel hostess. If she could melt into a puddle beneath the table, she would.

"You boys know that is not acceptable talk at my table. And while we're at it, I'd like to know who left that whole tray of tiramisu on the kitchen counter last night?" She looked around the table for the offending culprit. Sophie finally understood what a volcano must feel like right before it erupts, with molten shame forcing its way up through her body, leaving its scarlet trail across her face.

"Mamma, what are you talking about?" Valentina said. "I put it away myself last night after dinner."

"Yes, well, this morning I found it on the kitchen counter. Whoever helped themselves to it didn't take care to be particularly neat with it either. It almost looked like someone put their face right in it and started eating away like a dog in a bowl of kibble. Not to mention there was tiramisu on the ground and on the counter. This is not a zoo, people. You need to be respectful of others."

Sophie tried to make eye contact with Lorenzo, but he refused to look her way.

"Maybe it was someone from the camera crew out on a late-night bender," Lorenzo said.

Sophie glared at him. How dare he blame her crew? Then again, shame on her for not owning up to the crime herself. She couldn't, though. Nevertheless, Lorenzo should man up and take responsibility for the whole thing. After all, it was his fault things got out of control. And that they were both so horny they didn't even think to put it away or clean up after themselves. Well, sure, she bore some responsibility as well, but he should cover for her out of respect for her status as a thoroughly humiliated houseguest who could never admit to his mamma that she didn't clean up her mess because she was desperate to fuck the woman's son.

Argh! She tried so hard to do everything by the book. This show was her baby. She had to get it right. Diddling with the woman's son was so not getting it right. She had to end this thing she'd started with Lorenzo and end it suddenly.

As soon as the awkward breakfast was done, she cleared her throat. "Uh, Lorenzo. I have a few things to discuss with you. About the show. Maybe you and I can sit down now to figure that out?"

The man looked like a desperate weasel trying to squirm out of the beak of a hungry hawk. Which didn't thrill Sophie one bit. After all, only hours ago he'd been buried so far inside her it was hard to tell where one of them stopped and the other began. Surely he wasn't going to play that stupid "on second thought" game, was he? Like what boys in tenth grade would do. Impossible that a man of his age would do that. Right?

He escorted her down the hallway and they tucked into a large storage room that held cases of wine set aside for family use.

"How could you have let that happen this morning?" Sophie hissed at him.

"What?"

"Uh, for starters, telling me to tell your brother to go fuck himself. That was so not cool. And for it to happen with your mother coming into the room. Do you know how badly that reflected on me? And then the tiramisu. Need I say more about the tiramisu?" She paused, flashing back to last night and the moment when the food went from a simple dessert to an instrument of sexual foreplay. She shook her head. *Must. Stay. On. Message.*

"It's not my fault you shouted it out in front of Mamma. You should have known better!"

Her eyes grew large, and her unrequited outrage hung in the air like the overwhelming scent of ozone before a summer storm.

"Oh, really? I should have known you were going to make me a pawn in your stupid fraternal war, just like your brother made me one by dangling me in front of you like a pork chop to a starving mongrel? What is wrong with you people that you treat your guests in such an offensive way?"

"Lighten up, cara. This is what families do."

"Don't cara me." She drilled her finger into his chest.

The same chest she'd fondled only hours earlier. "And maybe your family does, but I can promise you I come from one seriously messed-up family, and even we don't do things like this."

The scowl on his face spoke volumes.

"And another thing. You could have grown a pair and stayed the night rather than sneaking out like some college girl avoiding the Sunday morning walk of shame. I thought you were old enough and mature enough to handle whatever it was that seemed to be happening between us. Clearly while I thought you were a man, you must really be all boy inside."

"Wait a minute, lady. I don't know where you got the idea that just because we had some fun in bed we were anything more than a fantasy fuck. Everyone knows this about Lorenzo Romeo: I do not do relationships. Period. Don't come looking for your happily ever after with me. Of course I'll be more than happy to make you happy— even ecstatic—for an hour or two in bed, but for life? That's not my thing."

"Well, fine," Sophie said. "Don't flip your shit on me. You can go ahead and be a stone-cold, selfish prick for all I care. I have one thing to say to you. It's something I learned from someone I can assure you is exceptionally good at it, being that I saw him in action my first day here. I hope you'll take it to heart: fottiti."

With that she turned and stormed out of the storage room, in a small way glad she wasn't going to have to pretend she wasn't interested in him only to keep up the ruse. Because the fact was, she hated the man and wanted nothing to do with him ever again.

Chapter Twenty-One

THE nice thing about Italians, Sophie thought, is that they take a good, long break in the middle of the day. It's civilized. By all accounts, it's a great time to have a much-needed lunch, take a nap, or catch up on a long, leisurely session of sex. It's the Italian way.

Sadly she was decidedly not catching up on sex with anyone, although she was thinking she might have to schedule ten minutes with that exceedingly loud battery-operated boyfriend of hers because right now tension was running high. Though not of the sexual variety. More like the "he'd better not get near me while I've got a baseball bat in my hand" type.

The rest of the day had been strained at best, though mercifully, Lorenzo made himself mostly scarce. He never even appeared at dinner, thank goodness. Out of sight, out of mind. Well, not really, but she could pretend as much.

Although Sophie was an American worker, while in Italy she was working Italian hours. Midday was time to chill out. She and Gisele had changed into bikinis and were lathering up their sunscreen poolside when Justin and Gareth arrived.

"Well look at the two of you," Gisele said. "I don't think I've seen you once since dinner the other night."

"Gareth's been taking me around the Tuscan countryside, giving me the grand tour."

Sophie raised her eyebrows. "Oh really? Sounds serious. Do I have to give Gareth the talk about how I keep a shotgun by the front door, and if he shows up for a date he'd best be respectful?" She winked at them.

"Ignore Soph, Gareth. She can be a bit of a smart-ass."

"Bit?" She laughed. "I'd say I'm one hundred percent Grade-A smart-ass, thanks. And I say that with pride." She gave him two thumbs-up. "But I'm glad you guys are having fun. At least someone is."

Justin pouted. "Awww, you're not, Soph? You seemed to be having fun at dinner the other night."

She rolled her eyes. "Not hardly."

"You mean to tell me you and loverboy didn't get it on after you sat on his lap the whole way home? I saw what you left behind after you got out of the car."

Gisele held her hand to her mouth. "No! Seriously?"

Justin nodded. "Hot Rod Lincoln poking out of that boy's pants. I admit to a fleeting moment of jealousy that it wasn't mine for the taking."

"It wasn't mine either so stop it!" Sophie tried to get away from the conversation by digging for a book in her bag.

"Wait, you mean to tell me you didn't end up doing squat thrusts in the cucumber patch?" He gave her a pronounced wink.

"You aren't serious. When you use phrases like that no one can take you seriously. Please reword that for human consumption."

"Well did you play a rousing game of hide the salami? Give the dog a bone? Hide the bishop? Hanky-panky?

Load the clown into the cannon? Shagging? Rumbusticating?"

"Is this some sort of thing where you try to wear down the suspect and eventually they spill their guts and admit to the crime?"

He nodded. "Pretty much."

"Okay, fine. I'll admit it. But you three are sworn to secrecy. And Gisele, that means you can't breathe a word of it to Tomasso, either, now that I know he's been trying to manipulate this whole thing. I want everyone to mind their own business and keep me the hell out of anything to do with the Romeo men. Or boys, as it is with some of them."

Sophie squirted some more sunscreen into her hand and began to rub it into her legs.

"Can't you talk and rub at the same time?" Justin said, anxiously.

"You are so impatient! Fine. I'll sunburn in order to yield to your titillation pleasure." She wiped the remaining lotion from her hands onto the towel so she could focus. "So the last thing on my mind was anything to do with him. I mean you guys saw him—he was obnoxious to me at dinner. To be honest, he's been obnoxious ever since I first had to deal with him."

She mentally wrestled with whether to start at the true beginning, but decided she didn't need to further humiliate herself on that one.

"And sure, he's been a jerk to me, although I'd be lying if I didn't admit there was some weird chemistry going on between us. Sort of disturbing, because not like I encouraged it. So the other night, I went into the kitchen to put my leftovers in the fridge, when what to my wondering eyes did appear but a huge pan of tiramisu that was calling my name."

Gisele squinted. "Tiramisu? The same one that Fabiana was asking about?"

Sophie groaned. "Ugh. Yes. One and the same."

Justin rubbed his hands together in glee. "The plot thickens."

"Let me tell you, she makes a seriously mean tiramisu. I'm just sayin'," Sophie added.

"Maybe we'd have known that but somebody left it out on the kitchen counter all night!"

Sophie held her finger to her lips for Gisele to be quiet. It appeared that only a few laborers were in the garden nearby but she didn't want to take a chance. Lord only knew what kind of spies Lorenzo had planted around the place and she didn't want to give him the satisfaction of being the object of her a) conversation and b) lust. Shame the latter wasn't going so well as of yet.

So there I am stealing a few fingers full of tiramisu—"

"You were sticking your hands right in there?"

"Yeah, well I knew you weren't going to have a chance to have any so what did it matter?" She cracked a smile. "Look, I was being a total gorging pig. And Lorenzo busted me. And in my defense, I'd had few glasses wine that night."

"And prosecco." Justin held up a finger as if to make a fine point.

"And limoncello," Gisele added.

"Ditto for the grappa," Gareth piped in. Sophie groaned. It was a wonder she hadn't passed out cold.

"Ugh, don't remind me. But Lorenzo was there and, guys, you know he smells amazing, right? And let's just say that I had it on good authority that he's got a smokin' hot body. He's somewhat impossible to not lust after, on a certain level. Besides, the tiramisu was delicious, so I held up a scoop for him. Which he licked obligingly off my fingers."

"Say no more. This is going to be beyond what my delicate ears can handle. I only hope that you didn't end up with tiramisu where the sun doesn't shine." Justin laid on a thick Southern accent as he pretended to fan himself like a virginal plantation mistress.

"Wait a second, Justin." Gisele held her hand up. "I want to hear every dirty detail. Continue, Soph."

Sophie shook her head at Justin. "As if you are some sort of prim-and-proper thing." She turned to Gisele. "One thing led to another and in the middle of the frenzy, we must've forgotten all about the tiramisu—"

"Are you kidding me? You had much more important things to concern yourselves with," Gisele said.

Sophie nodded. "If you only knew the half of it."

"Well, did you guys?"

"Did we?"

"Do the nasty?"

"We did a lot of nasties. Over the course of several hours. It was amazing. Except that he's one of *those* guys." She lifted her sunglasses onto her head to look around at her friends, ensuring they knew what she meant.

"Those guys?" Gareth said.

She pouted as she put her sunglasses back on. "The type who get buyer's remorse. At the time, by God, the man was having the time of his life. I can assure you that. But by dawn's early light? He'd morphed into the king of chicken shit."

They all laughed.

"I have to ask you," Justin said, leaning in. "Based on what I saw after you moved off his lap. And I ask this because I always like to hear about legends. Was his as epic as it looked like it could be?"

Sophie rolled her eyes. "I mean I'm not the world's foremost expert on the size of a man's penis. Sure I've had my share, but it's not like I'm a porn actress and see a new one each day. But yeah, his is just right. Long and thick and pretty much perfect." She closed her eyes, remembering how perfect it was.

It was a shame a precision tool like that was wasted on a perfect tool like him.

Chapter Twenty-Two

LORENZO was starving. He'd gone for a long run to clear his head and hadn't realized how hungry he was. As he worked his way back toward the house, he took a shortcut that followed behind the pool, which meant he was out of sight to anyone lounging poolside.

As he approached the area, he recognized her voice. And what he heard stopped him dead in his tracks.

"But yeah, his is just right. Long and thick and pretty much perfect."

She's honestly talking to them about my cock? He frowned. *At least she was impressed with it.*

And here he'd been worried she'd maybe come after him in his sleep with a cleaver, she was that pissed at him.

His ears perked up as they continued to talk.

"Would you ever fuck him again?" *He thought that was Gisele talking.*

Silence descended on the conversation. "Would I fuck him again?" Sophie said. "Well… Like I said, it was a damn-near-perfect cock. Too bad the owner was a near-perfect *culo.*"

She called him an asshole?

They all laughed. "Honestly there is some scary chemistry between us. I'd almost be afraid I wouldn't be able to resist. But for my own self-respect, remind me of this: I'd sooner never have sex again than have it with that rat bastard."

Touché. He blew that one. The hottest woman he'd bagged in eons, sleeping right across the hall from him. And she was now officially off-limits. And for what? Because he was so adamant about his single status and proud of it? Considering what he'd be missing out on, it was beginning to seem sort of stupid. Good thing there were other women he could snap his fingers for and they'd come running.

Culo. He wasn't an asshole. He simply didn't want to get hurt. And the easiest way to avoid that was to not put yourself out there to begin with.

He slipped back into the house by way of the front door to avoid being seen by the group bad-mouthing him poolside. As he entered, he happened upon his mother, who was sitting in the living room working on a needlepoint project. She was always making things like knitting baby blankets for orphans or stitching needlepoint seat cushions for the church.

"Lorenzo, caro, pull up a seat," his mamma said. "We haven't talked in a while."

"Of course, Mamma."

"We'll get Allegra to bring you something to eat."

"I'd love that." Allegra had been nanny, housekeeper, tender to broken hearts, and all-around invaluable non-blood-relative family member his whole life. Even now she remained with the Romeo family, tending to whatever their needs might be.

"So talk to me about what is up with you these days. I've noticed that you're quite on edge lately. Particularly since the arrival of Sophie Pellegrino. And I'd like to know what's up with that. Because you're not being a shining example of good manners, you know?"

He sighed. "I'm sorry, Mamma. I'll try harder."

"It's not a matter of trying harder, tesoro. It's a matter of trying from your heart."

"You know I don't operate from my heart."

"And you don't see that as a problem ever?"

"Look, Mamma. You of all people should be well aware of the hazards of placing your heart in someone else's hands. So simple for them to squeeze the blood from it, isn't it? Look at what Papà did to you!"

His mother looked at him, confusion in her eyes.

"I've seen a look that comes over you when you've been with Sophie. Maybe it would be good for you to get to know her better. She seems like a nice young woman. She's an Italian girl, you know."

God, did this mean his mother picked up on the look of unrequited lust that glimmered in his eyes for her?

"Thanks, but I don't need you matchmaking for me, Mamma. I know what's out there. I know what my options are. And most importantly, I know what's not right for me."

She patted him on the knee before he stood to go. "Promise me you'll keep an open mind. I think something about this one is different."

The next morning Sophie was up before sunrise, unable to sleep. This whole Lorenzo thing was gnawing at her, but she was at least going to get a move on and do something with her day rather than fritter the morning away ruminating about him.

She threw on a pair of shorts, a sports bra, and wifebeater, then grabbed her shoes, hoping to fit a run in before the sun became too hot.

She stopped for a quick espresso in the dining room, where she ran into Fabiana.

"Sophie! Cara mia. Up so early?"

Sophie cringed to hear yet another person referring to her as cara. In her mind, that word belonged to Lorenzo. Yet of course if he dared call her that now she'd slug him.

"Buon giorno, Fabiana. I thought I'd get an early start on things and go for a run around the property. It looks to be a gorgeous day." Fabiana's handbag hung from her shoulder. "You're heading out early as well."

"Would you care to join me, Sophie? I'm on my way to the market in Santa Romeo. It might get a little crazy in there this morning since artists are preparing for the Infiorate. But I think you'll enjoy seeing how their work is coming together, not to mention the market is wonderful. You can really get a feel for a place when you've had a chance to slowly wander around an open-air market."

Sophie thought for a moment. On the one hand, it might be awkward being alone with Lorenzo's mother under the circumstances. But she was none the wiser and she was a lovely woman, so why not? And what an awesome way to start her day. She could run any old time. This would be a unique Italian experience.

"I'd love to join you—thank you so much for thinking

of me! If you can give me a minute, I need to run back to the room to get my wallet and sunglasses."

"Take your time, cara. I'll be here waiting for you."

"And it's okay if I look a bit bedraggled? I haven't showered yet or anything."

Fabiana waved her hand dismissively. "You look beautiful the way you are, *stella*."

On her way back to her room she pulled out her phone and opened the Google translate app and typed in the word "stella." She'd learned her lesson after the great fottiti episode. She scrolled her finger along the word that came up. "Star," she said aloud. What a lovely little term of endearment. "Star. I'm a star. I'll have to remember that. It will be my daily affirmation: *Sono una stella*. I am a star."

Even if she didn't feel like a star, she was going to be one, come hell or high water.

Chapter Twenty-Three

SOPHIE knew the Italians operated on an entirely different schedule than they did back home. Stores were open earlier; they closed for a large chunk of time midday and opened again, often later into the evening. Of course that meant mealtime was always much later. The pace of it felt surprisingly right, though. Back home, it was go-go-go from the minute your eyelids opened till the moment your head hit the pillow well after midnight. There was something to be said for the more life-affirming way Italians chose to live. More relaxed. Or what was it someone had said to her? *Calme.* Calm down, relax. Certainly a lifestyle she could embrace. Didn't they even call it *la dolce vita?* The sweet life indeed.

Fabiana pulled her car into a lot at the base of the hilltop town and they took an elevator up to the village. So clever how they got around the obstacles of these hilly areas. It would have been a bitch climbing up a good mile along the roadside, especially since you weren't allowed to park or drive in villages unless you were a resident.

"Normally I can park inside the walls of Santa Romeo," Fabiana said, "since it is our family namesake and it wouldn't be here without our ancestors. But between the busy market and the preparation for the Infiorate, parking will be at an even greater premium. I'd rather leave it for someone who needs it more than I do."

If only Lorenzo inherited a little of the nice gene from his mother, the world would be a better place.

They wandered through row upon row of vendors selling their wares—everything from kitchen utensils, toys, and clothing to fresh local produce and cheeses. Fabiana stopped to chat with each of her favorite vendors, being sure to introduce Sophie as she did.

Sophie was starting to pick up a bit more Italian. She'd learned some basics growing up in an Italian household. Her grandmother never did speak much English, so Sophie grew to understand conversational words simply from eavesdropping on her elderly nonna when she'd gossip with the other neighborhood nonnas. Yet here, live and in person with actual Italians chattering away, it wasn't as easy to grasp much of what was being said.

Fabiana took Sophie to a booth that was selling porchetta sandwiches.

"You must try one," she said, paying for one for each of them. "You can't leave Toscano without having had one."

Sophie took a bite and moaned at the delicious merging of flavors, the warm, juicy pork rolled into a medley of herbs and spices. Street food at its finest. They even had some gelato afterward, which was weird—Sophie had eaten more food by nine in the morning than she'd had in an entire day back home. And she didn't even think twice about the calories. This was Italian living at its finest.

"Angelina!" Fabiana said as she waved to a small woman with short gray hair who was approaching.

"Fabiana! I was hoping I'd run into you."

"Me as well," she said. "I wanted to ask you about a conversation I had with Lorenzo. It left me scratching my head, and I thought maybe you could shed some light on it."

"Is everything all right with Lorenzo?"

She waved her hand. "Oh, he's fine. He's Lorenzo, as always. Heart of gold encased in steel."

The two of them laughed.

"But he wasn't like that as a little boy," Angelina said. "Remember, he was such a sensitive child. Always concerned with everyone's feelings. You remember when your dog was killed by the wild boar? All the children wailed, except Lorenzo. Instead of crying, he comforted his siblings."

Sophie perked up her ears. Lorenzo? Employing empathy? Impossible.

"I do remember, which is what troubles me," Fabiana said. "The other day he told me that I of all people should know what happens if your heart gets broken. He said look at what Papà did to me."

"What he did to you? He loved you with all of his heart." Angelina paused, lost in thought. "Ahhh… but when he died, you were so heartbroken."

"Yes, although that wasn't Giovanni's fault. He didn't set about to deliberately hurt me."

"But remember Lorenzo at the time, cara. He was the one who sat by your side. Who wrapped his arms around your trembling shoulders. Who scratched your back so you could fall asleep after hours of crying. Lorenzo saw what happened to someone who loved so much then lost. It left its mark on him."

A look of awareness came over Fabiana's face. "Mio

Dio! My son isn't heartless. He's just terrified of losing his heart, he was scared seeing what it did to his mamma."

Angelina smiled. "That boy has a heart as big as a mountain. I never bought all that gossip about him and his roaming eye. I think his problem has long been that he's a frightened little boy in a man's body."

Sophie sighed. Didn't she even call him a boy in a man's body? Or something like that. Hit the nail on the head but didn't understand the reason for it. Poor Lorenzo. Her heart sort of ached for that boy who lost his father and had to try to piece his mother back together again. Bless his heart. He probably couldn't even recognize this was the root of his detachment issues. Geez, what a good therapist could do for him.

"Mi dispiace," Fabiana finally said to Sophie. "My children call me the *chiacchierone*—the chatterbox—because I love to gossip with my friends when I go into the village."

Sophie smiled. "No apologies needed. I'd happily join you in the gossip if I knew anyone and had some good dish to share."

"Stick around long enough, I'm sure we can catch you up."

"I love that word. How did you say it? Chiaccherione? It's sort of mellifluous. Rolls off the tongue."

"It comes from the word 'cluck,' *chiocciare*. The gossip is clucking like a chicken. I suppose it's an insult although I don't take it as one."

Sophie laughed. "I'd be honored if someone called me a chiaccherione."

Fabiana reached her hand out. "Come, sweet Sophie. We have work to do. But first, let's go see what Domenico has been up to with his flower art."

Fabiana tucked Sophie's hand beneath her arm, an affectionate gesture that made Sophie feel all warm and tingly. Having grown up with a mother somewhat void of affection, it was a new sensation. She was growing to care for Fabiana—she was welcoming, charming, and thoughtful. And not only was she a mother to so many, she was a surrogate mother to whoever needed her. So that was what it was like for people who had real moms, like those TV moms who seemed so perfect. She made a mental note to remember to be that kind of mom if she ever got married and had children.

Sophie couldn't get enough of Santa Romeo either, with its old-world charm. Strolling along the cobbled streets, she felt at home amongst the warm, limestone facades, the terra-cotta tiled roofs, the obligatory imposing cathedral on the piazza in the center of town.

When she stopped looking up at the majestic spires, she averted her gaze to see what everyone had been talking about: stunning murals composed only of flower petals. Floral murals! That made her laugh. She turned her head this way and that, trying to get a glimpse of the works in progress. It was still hard to discern what many of the final portraits would look like, but she could see forms taking shape, complete with shading and details, such as the musculature in a depiction of Jesus on the cross. It was spectacular. One mural had a woman with long, flowing blond hair that stretched the length of the roughly fifteen-foot-long mural. Breathtaking.

Not to mention the intoxicating scents wafting through the air: wild thyme, the licorice aroma of anise, the sweet smell of rose, the heavy perfume of jasmine, and the peppery tang of fresh basil.

They found Dominico hunched with a team of helpers over a brilliantly colored mural replica of the famed Botticelli painting *Birth of Venus*, which depicts Venus naked on a shell along the shoreline, a metaphorical depiction of the birth of love and spiritual beauty as a driving force of life. That the man had the vision to craft such an iconic image from mere flower petals, leaves, and herbs was hard to fathom.

"Dominico, I had no idea the breadth of your talent," Sophie said. "This is truly spectacular."

He stood up and wiped his hands on his pants. "Thank you for noticing. It's

something that makes me happy. I get a thrill being able to share it with others."

"How do you keep the petals from blowing away?"

"Depending on the weather, we'll install canopies to protect our work from the elements. With the forecast being for perfect temperature and no wind or rain, we've been working without cover. We keep the flowers fresh by spraying frequently. That way they don't dry out."

"The Romeo family always seems to be full of surprises," she said. "Your brother Tomasso is such a gifted woodworker."

"And Mamma here, she does some pretty mean embroidery." He beamed at his mother and she poked him in the ribs as he gave her a huge bear hug.

"My boys love to tease me." Her eyes twinkled. "And speaking of my boys, look who we have here." She extended her arms to greet none other than Lorenzo. Great. The last person on the planet she wanted to see.

Chapter Twenty-Four

LORENZO frowned the minute he saw Sophie with his mamma and brother. He had been feeling a little bad for how things had ended with them, but he saw no other way. Unfortunately he was having a much harder time dismissing memories of their intimate moments together. He'd worked hard to avoid being anywhere near her because the instant he saw her, he could only envision her naked as he entered her from behind. Not a great thing to fantasize about while standing in front of his mother and Dominico.

"Lorenzo, amore, let me get a picture of you two together." She pulled him over toward Sophie, who looked like she was about to throw up. She pushed him shoulder to shoulder with her and squeezed his cheeks, forcing him to smile.

"Mamma, *per favore*." Please. Stop the madness, woman. He tried to wave her away to no avail.

"Wait," his mother said. "Put your arm around Sophie's waist."

He rolled his eyes but she reprimanded him. "*Sbrigati*, Lorenzo." Hurry up.

He lifted his arm as if it was made of heavy iron and reluctantly reached it around Sophie's waist until they were hip to hip. He was grateful to have a layer of fabric protecting his legs from touching her exposed one, so long and lean and perfect in those running shorts. He started thinking about those legs when they were wrapped around his hips as he pistoned into her warmth. *Merda.* He needed to get away from this scene of torture, prontissimo.

His mother pulled her iPhone from her handbag and started fumbling with it as the two of them stood there, stock-still. She held up the phone and started pushing things on the screen.

"Mamma, you're videotaping us." Lorenzo rolled his eyes when he heard the recording tone ding. "Slide the screen till you get to the photo one."

His mother seemed to be taking an eternity to do this and yet still, not a word from either of them toward the other.

"You two can talk amongst yourselves while I figure this camera out," she said with a wink.

"It's fine," Sophie said.

"I've got things to do, Mamma," Lorenzo said, accidentally pulling Sophie toward him as he leaned down to glance at his wristwatch to check the time. Of course that meant her tits were about eye level. And in turn, his dick came to life in his very tight jeans. Could the day get any worse?

"Okay, finally, I think I've figured it out. Are you ready? *Sorridi!*" she said, encouraging them to smile for the camera.

She finished taking the shot and instantly Lorenzo dropped his arm away from Sophie. Fabiana inspected the photo she'd just taken and looked up at them. "Uh-uh." She wagged her finger at him. "I need another one. You look like you'd rather be at the morgue than have your picture taken with this pretty woman. I want you to look alive. You're a handsome young man, she's a beautiful girl. Lean over and give her a kiss on the cheek for the camera, would you?"

Lorenzo growled. "Really? Must we? I have things to take care of."

"Truly, Fabiana, there's no need for this. I'm good without it. No need for the memories to be preserved."

But Fabiana was hearing none of it. "On the count of three: uno, due, tre. And you'd better kiss her on the cheek, Lorenzo, or no tiramisu for you tonight."

With that, Sophie burst out laughing as did Lorenzo, in time for Fabiana to snap off a few shots.

She looked down to see her handiwork, smiling. "See, now this is what a good picture is. I should be a professional." She winked at them both but by then they'd already inched away from one another. "I'll send you both the picture so you can save it to show your grandchildren one day."

Lorenzo blanched. Sweet *Gesù*, she had it out for him.

Lorenzo was in the subterranean wine cellars in the new building when his mother wandered in later in the day.

"Tessaro," she said. "We should talk."

He knit his brows. "Everything okay, Mamma?"

She ran her fingers through his thick hair. "Of course.

Everything is wonderful."

She looked around the vaulted cellar, so peaceful yet so majestic it gave the sense of being in some sort of cathedral. The terra-cotta walls and honey wood floors warmed the place despite the chill in the air.

"This," she said, her arms outspread. "This was the brainchild of Giovanni Romeo."

He nodded. "It is indeed."

"Your father who loved deeply and cared deeply and gave me the gift of seven wonderful children. It was almost as if he knew he needed to leave a lot of himself behind to hold me in good stead once he was gone."

"I thought you said we were a pain in your behind." He winked at her and she gave him a swat on his bottom.

"Lorenzo, *mio figlio*. My son. I don't have words to express my deep regret that my sorrow at losing your father affected you as negatively as it has. I truly had no idea that you were afraid to love for fear of losing that person." She sighed deeply. "It was wrong of me to lean on you back then. You were only a boy. And I was so lost without your father, I wasn't thinking clearly. There were so many characteristics of you that reminded me of Giovanni, I guess maybe it was comforting to be comforted by you. It was almost like it was him, one step removed."

She began to pace the floor.

"The thing is, my sweet boy, I would go through the pain of losing him all over again, if only to have him with me again. That's the power of love. Yes, there is pain in loss. But there is much more pain in never having had that love because you've denied yourself the joy. Every day I spent with your father is a day I've treasured, not one I've regretted."

Lorenzo shook his head. He didn't want to have this discussion anymore. "I understand."

"I don't think you do, Lorenzo. I've seen you around Sophie Pellegrino. I can tell you're holding back with her. I didn't understand why until now—that it was my fault, really. And I can't be happy knowing that you won't allow yourself the happiness of loving a woman simply because you had to bear witness to my heartache. She's a beautiful, smart, strong woman, my son. She's not like the many forgettable girls you've flipped through like a bored person with an old magazine in a doctor's waiting room." His mother looked pointedly at him. "I can see it in your eyes when you're near her. I see the yearning that is hidden behind that wall you've conveniently built up to protect yourself. But that wall is doing nothing other than hurting you and depriving you of happiness." She shook her head.

"Lorenzo, life is sweetest when shared with those you love. I hope you'll think long and hard about this, and give Sophie a chance before it's too late."

She leaned forward and kissed him on his forehead. "*Ti amo.*" I love you. "And I think deep down, you love her." She pulled back, her hands on his shoulders. "It's not often in life you have the chance to fall in love with someone special, someone who makes you a better person. Someone you yearn to spend your waking hours with." Her eyes glistened as she continued. "When you find that person, you need to seize the moment. Because that is the thing you should have learned about losing Papà: you only have the time you have to revel in that love."

Chapter Twenty-Five

LORENZO hated when he was wrong and she was right. Always had. Especially when he had no idea how to rectify the situation. He'd hurt Sophie by his actions. How could she ever trust that he'd not do something like this again?

He stood at the bar in the tasting room, swirling wine in his glass mindlessly. He pulled out his phone and opened to the picture of him with Sophie that his mother had sent him. He pressed on the image and spread his fingers to widen it so he could stare at her up close. He scrolled around the image, staring at her body, not wanting to admit he'd practically committed it to memory that first afternoon when he caught her with the vibrator. He scrolled along her long legs and closed his eyes as he remembered them spread wide and draped over his shoulders at some point that night.

He'd hardly known the woman yet she'd gotten under his skin so quickly. How could that be? And he would be lying to himself to say otherwise. He'd been with plenty of women in his life. Not a one ever elicited such feelings, even extreme emotions, for that matter.

Suddenly he had an idea.

He pulled up his brother's phone number and called it. "Mio fratello," he said. "I need your help."

Sophie, Justin, Gareth, Tomasso, and Gisele piled into a car right after dawn to make the short trip to Santa Romeo.

"In order to wake you up, I'm going to tell you a little more detail about the Infiorate," Tomasso said. "For instance, did you know that it's the children from in and around the village who are tasked with collecting all of the flowers and herbs for the floral carpets?"

"Why do you call them carpets?" Justin asked.

"They're spread across the ground all over the town. And will eventually be trod upon by the bishop. While the works are being created, usually the teenagers hold vigils all night long to protect them from any harm—that even includes a stray cat walking across them. The teens take turns sleeping and also working on their designated squares, applying leaves and petals where needed to fulfill the artists' demands. The artists might have the vision, but they need the manpower of the town to execute it. That's the beauty of this event." Tomasso smiled. "It pulls together people from different political beliefs, people who might have been having a property dispute or feuding over a woman or any such thing, and they have to work side by side to achieve a goal."

"World peace through flowers. I'm down with that," Sophie said, half-asleep still.

"So depending on the weather forecast, if it will be

cold or windy or rainy, the men will set up canopies to protect the works in progress," he continued. "Regardless, they'll string lights so that everyone can work round the clock. All night long, women will bring sweets and espresso to help workers stay awake. Meanwhile, old men will stand by with spray bottles to refresh the petals and keep them from drying out."

"Damn, they've thought of everything," Gisele said. "I wish I could run my feet through them."

"Sorry, that's reserved for the bishop. That's why we're coming early before the crowds swell to ridiculous proportions, which they will in an hour or so. This way we can wander the village and see all of the works before it's impossible to do so."

Tomasso continued steering down the road that led into Santa Romeo. "At noon, the bells of the cathedral toll, and the bishop will emerge, led by a brass band and flanked by a huge golden canopy held by four young men. The bishop carries the Holy Host high above his head as his procession wanders through town, going from one piazza to another, parading atop the floral carpets, flower petals scattering to the wind as the bishop's vestments drape across the designs."

"It must be heartbreaking for those artists to see their work whisked away so quickly. All that effort, and it's gone." Sophie snapped her fingers.

"It's probably a little bit painful for all involved," Tomasso said. "There is fierce competition to win and strict rules: paints are forbidden as is anything other than plant matter, primarily flower petals. Same with chemical preservatives. They're not even supposed to use dried flowers—judges reward the use of the freshest blooms.

And the prize money isn't much, split between the entire team that has assembled the carpet. The reward is really for bragging rights. But many of the artists are doing this for a higher cause, for religious zeal or purely a passion for whatever cause they've chosen to depict in their work."

It was early enough that Tomasso parked on a back street in the village so they could avoid too much walking. They walked toward the center of the main piazza, renamed Piazza Giovanni after Giovanni passed away years ago.

They gasped at the magnificent works spread out across the piazza.

"This is unbelievable," Gisele said. "I don't understand how anyone can make something so spectacular out of mere flowers."

"Right? As if the flowers aren't beautiful enough on their own." Sophie nodded.

They came upon a smaller floral mural of an elderly woman spread across the ground, her smile bright and beaming. "Oh, look," Justin said, giving Gareth's hand a squeeze. "It says here this is a tribute to the artist's late mother, who passed away this year."

Sophie wiped a tear from her eye. "How sad she didn't live to see it. She would be over the moon that her son or daughter created such a work of art."

"Such a moving tribute," Gisele said, her eyes glassy with tears.

Soon they found Dominico, still putting the finishing touches on his mural.

"Ahhh, Sophie. At last! We've been waiting for you."

Sophie squinted her eyes. "Me?"

He stood up and crooked his finger toward her. "Andiamo." Let's go. He led her down an alleyway between an old convent and the large cathedral, shifting here and there to avoid more spectacular floral carpets. They passed by a small playground and eventually came to a stop at the end of a dead-end street.

"It's the only place we could find that had any space left. And only because the bishop wasn't going to trek through a stand of trees to get to the next street." He grinned. "Oh, and by we, I mean me and Lorenzo."

A puzzled look fell across Sophie's face. *Lorenzo?*

She no sooner thought his name than he stepped out from behind a tree and walked toward them, holding up a sign of some sort.

"What's this all about?" Sophie wrinkled her nose, confused about what the hell was happening.

"Look down, Soph," Gisele said, pointing toward a floral mural that was probably ten feet wide by ten feet across.

Sophie gasped. Her eyes grew wide. "Wait a second. I don't understand." She shook her head, baffled about why Lorenzo was here and what he was doing. And why that?

Before her was a rendering of the image that Fabiana had taken of her and Lorenzo—when neither one of them wanted anything to do with the other. Well, technically not, but deep down? Maybe more than either cared to admit.

She looked up to see Lorenzo holding up a sign.

"Can you ever forgive me, Sophie Pellegrino?" It said. He dropped it, revealing another sign.

"I didn't mean to hurt you. I was so afraid of hurting myself I failed to worry about your feelings." He dropped the cardboard sign, making way for the next.

"Despite myself, I think I'm falling in love with you, cara." He dropped the sign, holding up the final one.

"Can we please start over?"

Sophie could barely read the last couple of signs. Her eyes had filled with tears. Never in her life had a man gone to such lengths to apologize to her before.

Lorenzo stood there, waiting for her response.

At last, Sophie took the handful of steps toward him, opened her arms wide, and wrapped them around his neck as she pressed her lips to his.

"A simple I'm sorry would have sufficed," she said when they finally broke the kiss.

"You're too special a woman to settle for ordinary, tessaro," he said.

"But how did you do this?" She motioned toward their floral portrait.

"I have a really kick-ass brother, for starters," he said. "I called him and he told me I had to round up a bunch of kids and help them gather all the colors we needed. It helped that there was a repository for cast-off flower petals that I was able to help myself to."

"So you were out in the countryside gathering flowers for me?"

"Until there wasn't a hint of daylight left. Meanwhile Dominico sketched out the image based on the photograph and I was able to round up some extra teens to help me as we filled in all of our designated squares."

"So you've been up all night long?"

He nodded. "You think I'm insane?"

"I think you're insanely amazing," she said.

The smell of lily of the valley wafted toward her, mingling with the savory scents of rosemary and sage.

"How on earth did you know I love lily of the valley? And those herbs?"

He cocked his head toward Gisele. "Let's just say I had my sources."

"Egged on by someone who wanted nothing more than to get you two together," Gisele said, playfully hitting Tomasso in the arm. "But trust me, I wouldn't let his ulterior motive win if I didn't think he was right on the money."

"Speaking of money," Tomasso said with a grin.

"Does this mean you're willing to retire your roamin' Romeo reputation?" Sophie lifted a brow and held tight to his hand.

His eyes twinkled. "It seems I learned the easy way that I much prefer the company of one Sophie Pellegrino than all the rest of the women I can find."

Sophie leaned over and kissed him and fake yawned. "Gee, I think maybe it's time to get you back to bed." She winked at him.

"I've got a lot of making up to do, don't I?" Lorenzo grinned.

"Not to mention a tiramisu to replace. Let's go. Time's a-wasting."

Thank you so much for reading *Silver Spoon Romeo!* I hope you enjoyed it! If so, please help others find this book:

1. Help other people find this book by writing a review.

2. Sign up for my new releases email so you can find out about the next book as soon as it's available and get fun giveaways.
http://eepurl.com/baaewn

3. Like my Facebook page.
www.facebook.com/jennygardinerbooks

And I love to hear from readers! Let me know what you think about my books! You can write to me at jenny@jennygardiner.net, and visit me on the web at www.jennygardiner.net.

Turn the page for a sneak peek of the next book in The Royal Romeos –**Blue-Blooded Romeo**

Blue-Blooded Romeo

Chapter One

THERE were times in her life that Stella Whitaker wished she could drop all pretenses of civility and speak her mind, and now was decidedly one of them. She'd spent the last several days with minimal sleep, working late into the night to complete her very first commissioned wedding cake for a bride getting married in Florence, Italy. After training for half a year at the elite French school of culinary arts, l'école Marondi, this was her first freelance project and she'd felt enormous pressure to succeed wildly with this project as she knew it would lead to more such jobs. The cake turned out exceptionally well, the bride was elated, and now she and her friend Alexa Philippe, who'd helped in transporting the masterpiece, had just gotten in line to board their flight back to Paris, where they were both about to begin their final class at Marondi, when the rudest man accosted Stella.

"*Scusi, signora.*" At first she thought maybe he was trying to make small talk, maybe even coming on to her. He was a handsome man: tall, with a broad chest that narrowed down to slim hips and—let's face it, it was impossible not to notice—a well-endowed bit of window-dressing. She could find plenty of ways to have a little fun with a guy like that. Instead he pointed at her boarding pass. "I'm afraid you're in the wrong line."

Stella squinted at him, wondering what business it was of his what line she was in, even though she was in the right one anyhow. As she looked at him she noticed he had the warmest brown eyes, with thick, long lashes that were, to be truthful, wasted on a guy. Though they looked damned good on him.

"Pardon?" she said, just wanting to get the ninety-minute flight from Milan to Paris over with so she could get some shut-eye.

He pointed again at her boarding pass. "*Ecco.* Here. Your boarding pass has you in 'zona quattro', zone four, but you're standing in the group for zone two. I'm afraid you need to go to the end of that line." He pointed to a queue that had a good thirty people in it. She counted the number of people in front of her in the current line in which she stood: only about six. She furrowed her brow. Who was this clown trying to police the airport line? So maybe she hadn't even looked at her boarding zone. What was the harm to him?

"Look, uh, *signor*," she said with emphasis. "My friend is in zone two and we're sitting together so I just got in line with her, assuming we'd be boarding at the same time. See, look at her boarding pass." She pulled the slip of paper from her friend's hands and held it up next to hers. "See, she's in seat 27 B and I'm in… I'm in…"

"Ah… It appears that was the confusion," he said. "You're in seat 14D."

Stella shook her head, her long, auburn waves dancing angrily across her shoulders. "Wait a minute. That's not right. We're supposed to be seated next to each other. What the—"

She was about to stomp over to the gate agent to fix the situation when an announcement was made that the flight was overbooked, which meant there would be no correcting of wrong seating assignments. Stella groaned. She still didn't understand why the guy had to be such a bossypants about it. Who died and made him the airport Stasi?

"What a coincidence! It looks like your friend and I are seated next to one another." The man combed his fingers through his thick, wavy dark hair. As much as Stella wanted to hate him for being such a buzzkill, he was awfully easy on the eyes. Even her overly-tired, void-of-a-good-night's-sleep eyes. She smiled one of those smiles you'd force onto your unhappy face after the nurse tells you you've gained ten pounds at your annual physical. Woo-hoo. Mr. Tall, Dark and Rigid gets to sit next to her friend and she's stuck in *zona quattro*, waiting forever to even get on the plane. Grrrr.

The man reached his hand out to Alexa. "Forgive my manners. I'm Dominico. Dominico Romeo." He turned and nodded as well to Stella and attempted to shake her head, which she ignored and instead crossed her arms and tucked her hands neatly beneath her armpits. *Zona quattro my ass.* Those airline zones were bogus, anyway. Every time she flew she got stuck in the one that was the last to board. It didn't matter where she sat on the plane, it was always the wrong damned zone. She just wanted to get on the plane, put her seatbelt on, have the plane take off, and finally settle in for a cat nap, which would have to suffice until she got back to her apartment.

Ugh, but the Nudge seemed to want to engage in conversation for some reason, which was plucking her last nerve.

"Yeah I had hoped to get a seat in first class, or at least business class, but I had to change flights at the last minute, and this was all they had."

Stella turned so that only Alexa could see her and pretended to be him talking, taking great joy in mocking him. Pretentious git. First class, schmirst class.

It was a shame she couldn't just tell the guy to go to hell, but that wasn't in her nature. She grew up in in an environment of conflict, with warring parents and warring step-parents and combative step siblings. She got quite practiced at hiding her animosity toward anyone who pissed her off, and she would do so yet again now. But still, it really irked her.

The gate agents announced that boarding was about to begin, and she stood there and watched as Alexa and Mr. Romeo—as if. He was about as Romeo as, well, hmmm. Actually he was sort of Romeo-handsome. And he was tragic—in that his personality obviously sucked. so that fit into the whole Romeo thing. Maybe he'd swallow some poison over the loss of a girlfriend, or whatever it was that Romeo guy did for Juliet, and she could take his seat on the plane. Did they serve strychnine on airplanes? She could send him a complimentary glass, on the rocks.

She stood there with the weight of her overloaded purse tugging on one shoulder, her computer bag on the other, watching as streams of people were being allowed onto the plane while her miserable zone four line stood, constipated. It took forever but finally they called her group, the last one, naturally. As she wheeled her carryon suitcase forward, a gate agent halted her just before scanning her ticket.

"I'm sorry, ma'am," she said. "You're only allowed one carryon item."

Stella frowned. "But that's all I have, this suitcase."

The agent pointed at her shoulders. "What are those?"

"They're my personal items!"

The gate agent pinched her lips shut and shook her head. She held up her pointer finger. "You're allowed one personal item. You're going to have to gate-check that suitcase."

Stella rolled her eyes. If she'd have just gotten on board before half of the city of Milan got on the plane, she'd have gotten away with it. But with all those people hauling all that luggage—most of them far more than she had—of course they were going to run out of room for carryon bags. Meanwhile she had all of her cake-decorating equipment in it in case of last-minute repairs. She couldn't afford to lose that because she couldn't afford to replace it, and it was her livelihood.

She heaved a sigh, grabbed the baggage check ticket from the gate agent, and relented.

It wasn't till she was on the plane, her bag long separated from her, that she remembered she'd tucked her breakfast into the rolling suitcase, in which she'd stashed some of her favorite Italian cheeses and salume. The icing on the cake was when she arrived at her seat to see she was sandwiched between a very large man whose leg-spread had spilled into her personal space by about ten inches and a child with a whooping-cough sound wheezing from his chest and a booger-encrusted nose whose middle name, she was sure, was "contagion".

At the rate things were going, this day could only get better. Or at least that was the optimistic take she was going to try to at least pretend to believe.

The upside was minus the rolling luggage, at least there was no last-minute desperate search for enough overhead bin space to jam her supersized carryon bag. But of course she had to wedge her laptop bag into a compartment in the far in the back of the airplane, which meant she'd have to wait for everyone else to get off the plane before she could walk the opposite direction of exiting passengers to recoup her bag. Lovely.

Once she finally settled into her seat, she carefully inspected the safety card. If there was to be a crash-landing, she wanted to know how to get out of this tin can in the air. Then, taking care to turn her head away from Typhoid Tommy next to her, she discovered the airline offered up a clever little app called Seat Chat, which allowed passengers to send messages to friends who were in other sections of the plane, using the screen in the headrest in front of them. At least she could communicate with her Alexa, if she couldn't be next to her. Far be it from that goon to have done the gentlemanly thing and let her sit next to her good friend.

She pressed the screen and typed in the seat number she wanted to send to.

"Hey girl. It's me. Stuck in passenger hell between a diseased boy determined to take advantage of my sleep-deprived immune system and share his germy air with me, and a man even more obnoxious than that cranky guy, the blue-blooded Mr. First Class jerk who kicked me out of line with you. What a jerk. I mean seriously. Who died and made it his business where I stood or what zone I entered through. I hate arrogant men like that. If he was actually a nice man, he'd have done the gentlemanly thing and offered to switch seats so you and I could sit together. Instead I'm sure he's sitting there looking all hot with his bedroom eyes and ugh, I couldn't help but look—with Italian men and those tight pants, how could you miss it? —he was seriously packing. Hope that thing doesn't get in the way of your seat haha! Now that makes me laugh—can you imagine him with his big old Italian Stallion cock spilling into your personal bubble? You'd best be careful or you'll be bitten by his love snake. In your personal bubble, no less. Omigod, I needed a good laugh after the past few hours. God I'm so freaking exhausted. I cannot wait to burrow under my duvet and crash out for about twenty-four hours. By now I'd be napping happily were it not for the jerk with the big dick. Or is he the dick with the big dick? Ugh, promise me you two won't fall in love in the next ninety minutes and then I'd have to be nice to him for the rest of my life and go to your wedding and then I'd have to admire the babies you made together even though every time I held your baby and stared into its eyes I would be reminded of what a complete prick your baby daddy was. But you're too smart for that. Maybe when he's not looking you can spit in his drink or something. I'd appreciate the passive aggressive gesture on my behalf. Oh well, I wish I had one of those hospital masks to cover my nose and mouth against the crud that little junior here is spewing my way."

She re-read it and laughed at her smartass comments. Oh, god, Alexa will be peeing her pants cracking up at this message. She hit the "send" button, put her seatback in its

upright position, and awaited take-off, hoping the rest of the day would be drama-free and filled with sweet dreams.

Blue-Blooded Romeo

coming July 25, 2017.

About the Author

Jenny Gardiner is the author of #1 Kindle Bestseller *Slim to None* and the award-winning novel *Sleeping with Ward Cleaver*. Her latest works are the *It's Reigning Men* series, featuring *Something in the Heir, Heir Today Gone Tomorrow, Bad to the Throne; Love is in the Heir, Shame of Thrones; Throne for a Loop; It's Getting Hot in Heir; A Court Gesture;* and her new Royal Romeos series, featuring *Red-Hot Romeo; Black Sheep Romeo, Red Carpet Romeo, Blue Collar Romeo, Silver Spoon Romeo* and the upcoming *Blue-Blooded Romeo*. She also published the memoir *Winging It: A Memoir of Caring for a Vengeful Parrot Who's Determined to Kill Me,* now re-titled *Bite Me: a Parrot, a Family and a Whole Lot of Flesh Wounds*; the novels *Anywhere but Here; Where the Heart Is*; the essay collection *Naked Man on Main Street*, and *Accidentally on Purpose* and *Compromising Positions* (writing as Erin Delany); and is a contributor to the humorous dog anthology *I'm Not the Biggest Bitch in This Relationship*.

Her work has been found in Ladies Home Journal, the Washington Post, Marie-Claire.com, and on NPR's Day to Day. She was also a columnist for Charlottesville's Daily Progress for over a decade, and is the Volunteer Coordinator for the Virginia Film Festival.

She has worked as a professional photographer, an orthodontic assistant (learning quite readily that she was not cut out for a career in polyester), a waitress (probably her highest-paying job), a TV reporter, a pre-obituary writer, as well as a publicist to a United States Senator (where she first learned to write fiction). She's photographed Prince Charles (and her assistant husband got him to chuckle!), Elizabeth Taylor, and the president of Uganda. She and her family and menagerie of pets now live a less exotic life in Virginia.

Visit Jenny at her website at www.jennygardiner.net where you can sign up for her newsletter, visit her blog, or find her on Facebook and Twitter. And every blue moon she'll post adorable pictures of her pets on Instagram as @thejennygardiner.